G̲
Two

Hammers and Crosses

Scott F. Nielsen

For Paul and Diane Nielsen, The best parents anyone could hope for, and my brother Bruce, and sisters, Julie Anne and Therese. You have all been there for me when I needed you, Jeg elsker jer alle.

1

Denmark 878 A.D.

Gardi was worried. Missionaries had been working in Denmark to convert people to the false god. Most of the Scandinavian people were still loyal to the Norse gods, but some people were wavering. So many had moved to England, There wasn't as much hope for them. His and Astrid's son Freki was over there, with 4 of his grandchildren.

He had found a Norse wife, a sweet girl named Alfdis. She provided him with 4 children, a boy Aesir, and 3 girls, Erika, Magna, and Kirsten. She was devoted to the Norse gods until they moved to England.

She had named her 3rd daughter Kirsten, which meant follower of Christ. She had converted to the false religion, and she was working on his son and grandchildren. There was nothing he could do. He could only make his feelings known when he visited, which wasn't often.

Brenda died in battle in 851. She gave him 6 children during that time. There were 5 boys, Baldur, Leif, Sveyn, Kol, and Bjørn. She had 1 girl who she named Lagertha.

They were all fierce warriors, but Lagertha was by far the most dangerous. Like her mother, she was a natural beauty, but equally ruthless. She was the youngest, born just a year before her mother's death.

This made her the same age now as Gardi was when he became immortal. In truth, he was 82, but in all other ways, he remained 28. She would start getting older than him soon.

She inherited Gardi's blond hair, but that was the only difference between Brenda and Lagertha. She was her mother's daughter. Her brothers were all great warriors, but they learned early to stay out of Lagertha's way.

One day when she was 9, she snuck out of the house and into the forest with a bow designed for a full grown man and one arrow. She came back an hour later with a 90 pound doe draped over her shoulders, skinned and gutted. She was always big for her age, and at 9 she was 5'9". Another time she saw another girl talking to a boy she liked and she punched her in the nose. When the girl fell to the ground, Lagertha sat on her belly, and with her knees on the girl's shoulders and started pummeling her face. A nearby adult stopped the attack, and had trouble pulling Lagertha off. The girl had 2 black eyes and a broken nose, but the parents didn't dare say anything.

Even though Gardi was the King at the time, and immortal, it was hard to tell which parent they were more scared of, him or Brenda.

Idun asked about Lagertha often. She showed keen interest in her fighting abilities, and marveled at the stories that Gardi would tell about her. She had told him that Thor was very impressed with her. Gardi considered this very high praise considering the source. Idun said that all of the gods had asked about her at one time or another, and that was why she continued inquiring.

    He never relayed the messages to her. He felt that she already had an oversized ego, and he didn't want to feed it. He loved her very much. She reminded him so much of Brenda it was scary.

    She had never married, nor had any kids. Truthfully, most men were scared of her. She had one long term relationship a few years back. His name was Gunnar. He was big, at least as big as Bolthor, and he was not scared of Lagertha. One day she caught him in bed with a slave. They had it out, and beat each other up pretty badly. She said that she would forgive him as long as it never happened again. All seemed normal, until a few weeks later, Gunnar 'went for a walk in the forest', as so many had in the past, never to return. Gardi knew the truth without speaking to Lagertha. He was proud of her. He wished that Freki had was some of that spirit. Since that time, men were wary of Lagertha.

    Margaret gave him a child, a daughter named Disa. Of course Brenda could never prove that the child was Gardi's, but she was furious. Gardi had to make Disa illegitimate. He gave Margaret protection during her pregnancy since she was a part of his household, but a few years after the child was born, she disappeared mysteriously in the forest. Gardi adopted Disa, but Brenda refused to acknowledge her. Shortly before her 5th birthday, she disappeared as well. Gardi wasn't stupid, he knew it was Brenda in both cases, but he couldn't prove it.

Astrid's death had crossed his mind on occasion, but none of the midwives suspected foul play. They all told him how upset Brenda was when she died. She and Brenda got along. Not like sisters, but far better than he had ever hoped for. Poisoning wasn't really her style anyway. If she was responsible for Astrid's death, she was as good of an actress as she was a warrior.

All of Brenda's kids stayed in Skagen. They wouldn't dream of moving to England or contemplating another religion.

Brenda had become very religious since marrying Gardi, and she passed it on to her children. Of course, they had an immortal man for a father. When they were old enough, he sat down with each of them and explained it. Knowing what Idun had done for him only made their convictions stronger.

Freki's family was different. They moved to England 8 years ago. The only time Gardi was over there was for raids. Freki was a decent warrior, but he just didn't have the killer instinct that Brenda's children did.

Perhaps it was because Astrid was his mother. After Baldur was born, Brenda didn't pay much attention to Freki. Gardi did the best he could, and he took Freki along on raids.

The difference was obvious from the beginning. Baldur was aggressive, and showed no mercy.

While Freki killed efficiently, he didn't like it. He was more inclined to show compassion to his victims. More than once Gardi had to tell him that he must kill an opponent, lest he recovers and comes after you.

Baldur was always looking for more Christians to kill. He frequently mocked Freki and called him a coward. It disturbed Gardi that Freki would just take it. He lacked the dignity to stand up for himself.

Freki was incredibly smart though. He seldom wanted to fight a battle, but he was more than willing to plan one. Gardi frequently took his advice, and was grateful for it. For this reason, Baldur did his best to get along. He knew how valuable Freki was, even though he didn't like to fight.

Gardi married again the same year that Brenda died. He didn't really want to, but Idun insisted. One of his directives from the gods was to create more descendants of Odin. He picked one of his shield maidens, Brunhilda. Idun told him that his wives should be as young as possible, for obvious reasons. Brunhilda was 17 when he married her. She was 44 now.

After explaining his instructions from the gods, she insisted that he take another wife...on one condition. Brunhilda got to pick her. She picked the blacksmith's daughter, Ama, who was sweet and meek like Astrid. She was 16 when Gardi married her in 853.

He figured that she picked Ama because she didn't appear threatening. Ama was cunning though, and she outsmarted Brunhilda on a regular basis. They became close, but Ama still routinely took advantage of her superior intelligence. Both were religious, and provided him with children.

He had 3 sons with Brunhilda she named them Floki, Dana, and Terje. She gave him one daughter and named her Magnilda. All were spectacular warriors.

Ama gave him 2 boys, Haakon, and Vali. She also had 2 girls, Siv, and Nanna. None of his children with Ama became Vikings, but they were all very smart. Haakon served as an advisor to the Earl, and Vali became a healer. The girls both married powerful men.

Gardi was preparing for another raid west. He would spend some time in France, then go over to England. He wanted to see Freki while he was there. It seemed that the situation was hopeless, but he had to try. The world was changing.

Was it too late for Freki? His grandchildren? He didn't care about Alfdis. He loved her because she was Freki's wife, but she was trying to pull his family away from the true gods. How could she not believe? Wasn't Gardi living proof?

The last time they talked, she told him that it was *Jesus* that had blessed him. He tried to reason with her, after all, Idun wasn't working with Jesus. She wouldn't hear a word of what he had to say. The worst part was that Alfdis influenced Freki so easily.

He was worried about their afterlife. He didn't want them to go to hell. She reasoned that they would go to heaven. *Her* god's heaven.

How could a man that let them nail him to a cross like a weakling ever protect them? Odin sacrificed an eye to gain knowledge, but he would *never* let them nail him to a tree! Not without a fight! Jesus even carried the cross to the top of the hill, so they could kill him! And forgave them as he died! What kind of god is that?

Freki had too much Astrid, and not enough Gardi. He loved him, and he had not given up on him, but this would be an uphill battle.

"What is on your mind, sweet Gardi?" she asked.

It was Idun.

"I am worried about Freki." he said. "His wife has too much influence over him. I fear that he may start to worship the false god."

"There are many that have succumbed to his tricks." she said. "So many have moved to England like your dear Freki, and unfortunately, that is just what they want. They want them close so that they can try to convert us. Do not underestimate Freki. Your blood flows through him, as does Astrid's."

"But is that enough?" he asked. "He can be weak willed. There are also my grandchildren to consider."

"You taught him well, Gardi." she said. "Although Brenda paid little attention to him, she was very religious. He grew up in a Norse household. He did not meet Alfdis until he was 25, and she was also religious before she was brainwashed. Your grandchildren have a solid foundation, and they are smart. Smarter than Alfdis. Do not give up on them."

"I have not." he said. "They are just so far away."

"Do you wish to move to England?" she asked raising an eyebrow.

"My home is here, and it always will be." he said.

"No it will not." she said. "It has been easy to this point, because people still believe in magic. There will come a time in the near future when you will *have* to move. They will stop looking at you as someone who has been blessed, and start looking at you as a heretic."

"How is that possible?" he asked.

"The world is changing, dear Gardi." she said. "People fear what they do not understand. Soon people will have to worship in private. As gods, we have seen this many times over the years."

"So what will we do?" he asked.

"It is our task to encourage belief in the *true* gods." she said. "It will not be easy. You have seen many changes just in the short time as we have been acquainted."

It was hard for Gardi to grasp the concept that 54 years was a short time. It all depends on your perspective, he thought.

She was right, of course. At the time he met Idun, everyone was religious and feared the gods. They mocked the Christians. *Their* god didn't make any sense. Now there were openly Christian Vikings. They were still outnumbered, but it never would have allowed it in the old days. If someone suspected a Viking of being Christian, he would have been executed without much of a trial.

"You said the 'near future'. How soon?" he asked.

"All I can tell you is to be ready, sweet Gardi." she said. "It will be good practice for the times to come. There will come a time when you are forced to move frequently to avoid detection."

"Why is that?" he asked.

"It is as I just spoke of, Gardi." she said. "The world is changing. You will become a pariah. People will no longer accept that you have been blessed by the gods. They will start to wonder why you do not age or die."

"The world *does* seem to be turning in that direction." he said.

"I would like for you to go and talk to a seer in Kattegat. To put your mind at ease about Freki." she said. "She is the best seer in Denmark. She works near the docks, everyone knows her."

"You know that I do not normally talk to seers." he said. "It seems that they only see one thing, that I am blessed with immortality. After they discover that, they talk about little else."

"She is not like that." said Idun. "Do you not trust me, Gardi? It will do you a world of good to talk to her."

"Of course I trust you." he said. "To be honest, most seers give me the creeps."

"Look past her appearance, dear." she said. "She will have much insight that will help you tremendously."

"Can you tell me more of the future?" he asked. "How soon will Scandinavia start to convert?"

"The future is what she is for." she said. "Be ready. The gods are looking over your family in England. Still, you must see her."

"Okay, I will make the trip down." he said.

"It will be okay, elsker." she said. "These are difficult times, Gardi. I understand your concern. The Viking Age is nearly over. Stay strong."

"Have you ever known me to be weak?" he asked.

"I have not." she said. "I only caution you to not be swayed by the false religion. Some of the strongest have converted."

"You can rest assured that I will not." he said. "I will talk to you after I speak with the seer."

"How is our girl?" she asked.

He knew that she was talking about Lagertha. It had become a routine during their meetings to discuss her.

"I am sure that you have been watching her." he said. "She never ceases to amaze me. She wants to be captain of a boat on the next raid."

"I am impressed." she said. "Will you let her?"

"She leaves me very little choice." he said. "She is the best warrior that I have. It is not even close. Kol and Bjørn will be disappointed since they are next in line, but even *they* would not dare to argue. They have a healthy fear of their sister. Everyone knows that she is the best warrior. It is even up for debate that she is better than me."

"Anything new in her love life?" she asked.

Gardi started laughing uncontrollably.

"When men see her they cross the road." he said. "If she looks at them, the vast majority run, and avoid the forest for weeks. I don't know if she will ever find a man that is brave enough to take a chance with her."

"But she is so beautiful!" she said. "Is there not *one* who can overlook her nature?"

"Like you said before, Idun, the world is changing." he said.

"It is sad." she said, frowning. "I must go, sweet Gardi. Do not worry about Freki. Go and see the woman in Kattegat. Everything happens for a reason."

"Thank you." he said. "I am grateful for your advice."

She gave him a light kiss on the cheek, and vanished into the forest.

He thought about Freki. He had seen him last year when they were in England.

It wasn't so much that he was worried that Freki would become a Christian, he worried more that he wouldn't have a god at all. That of course was preferable to him worshipping the false god, but just barely.

His wife had already converted, and she was devout. He worried more about that. Freki was incredibly smart, yet he was just as stubborn. He needed to get him back where he belonged.

He didn't know how to do that. He remembered a conversation that they had when he was over there.

"The people are different over here, dad." he said. "My friends know so much. I'm learning a lot."

"Have you been to that church with her?" he asked.

"Yes, she makes me go." he said. "I don't believe it, it's even more far out there than our gods."

"Our gods are far out there now?" he asked.

Freki started laughing.

"Are you serious? One supposedly controls the weather. Another gave up an eye to gain knowledge, well, actually he just gave up his eye for a drink from Mimir's Well." he said. "Did it work? Who knows?

Nobody has ever seen him! Another is a trickster that plays cosmic jokes on mankind. Another rides in a chariot pulled by cats, and has a cloak of falcon feathers so she can fly. Can you honestly tell me that the Norse gods are not fictional? Really? How can you be so naïve? "

"I have seen far more than you have, son." he said. "Have you forgotten that I have intimate contact with Idun? Look at me! I'm an 81 year old man! Can you explain that?"

"In theory." he said.

"Please. Tell me your theory." he said. "I'm dying to know."

"It is possible that you came in contact with some undiscovered substance that retarded your aging process." he said. They are discovering new things every day."

"Who is being naïve now?" he asked.

"Oh, come on!" he said. "If you only knew the things that we study over here, you would know that I'm right. Just keep an open mind, dad!"

"Funny, I was about to tell you the same thing." he said.

"What are you worried about?" he asked. "I'm not converting to *her* god."

"I'm worried about your afterlife, son." he said.

"Well, no worries, dad." he said. "We die, and that's it. So you can relax. Don't worry about your alleged gods. They have been talked about for so long that people actually believe in them now."

"It's not just talk." he said. "I wish I could show you."

"I wish you could too, dad." he said. "I'm always looking for new experiences. But that's never going to happen. *They're not real.*"

He could see that it was useless to try to convince him. But Freki was his *son*. He couldn't very well give up on him either. Another time, he thought.

But that other time never came. He left it like that. His son not believing. *That* was the hardest part. He didn't push hard enough. It was his fault.

* * *

He docked his boat and went ashore. The market was teeming with people. Gardi had never liked crowds. It was one of the things he loved about Skagen.

"Where is the seer?" asked Gardi.

"Third tent past the blacksmith on the right." replied a fisherman.

The one thing that he *did* enjoy about Kattegat was that nobody recognized him. He was just another ordinary man.

He entered the tent, and the seer gestured to a nearby chair. She wasn't unattractive like most of them. There was a scar starting on the bottom of her left cheek, passing through both of her eyes, and ending at her right temple.

"Do you know why I am here?" he asked.

"I know that Idun sent you, and that is all." she replied. "What can I do for you?"

"It is about my son." he said. "I worry about his afterlife. He has moved to England, and his wife has converted to the false religion."

"Freki will be okay." she said. "He is not as meek as he appears. He just finds it absurd to fight. He feels that it makes him look intellectually weak. He will be fine, Gardi."

Idun was right, she *was* good. She seemed to know everything.

"How do you know his name?" he asked. "How do you know *mine*?"

"Do you not recognize me, father?" she said.

Idun told him to look past her appearance, and that's what he did. She looked vaguely familiar. Why did she call him father? It finally dawned on him. She looked older of course, but just like her mother, when he imagined her without the scar. He shook his head in disbelief.

"Disa?!" he asked.

2

He was bewildered that she had somehow survived whatever Brenda had done to her. He quickly did the math. She would be 53 years old now.

"But...how?" was all he could get out.

"She took me deep into the woods. She gave me this." said Disa, running a finger along her scar. "The day she blinded me, I saw clearly for the first time in my life. She talked the whole time, she said things that no little girl should ever hear. She said that I would never find my way back, and if I didn't starve to death, the wolves would get me. I guess her twisted morals told her that she could not kill a little girl, but it was okay to leave me to die."

"But how *did* you survive?" he asked. "

"Like I said, on that day I saw clearly for the first time in my life. All of my other senses immediately became stronger. I gained a very strong second sight. She was right, the wolves *did* get me." she said. "They protected me, and fed me. I learned to walk without traditional vision, by using my ears and nose. I lived in the forest for 26 years, until I knew she was dead. I considered introducing Brenda to my new friends, but I knew that it would only hurt you. I do not blame you, father. I know all about you. You were fated to marry Brenda and have children with her."

"Your mother was a wonderful woman." he said. "She didn't deserve what happened to her. If I know Brenda, she made her suffer greatly."

He immediately regretted saying this, because he figured it would upset her more.

"I know what happened to Margaret." she said. "I also know what happened to Astrid."

He was shocked. Idun said she was the best seer in Denmark. Did he even *want* to know? Did he dare ask? He knew that she killed Margaret and Disa…well, apparently *not* Disa, but he didn't think that she would harm Astrid.

"I can see that you are apprehensive about this." said Disa. "I should not have mentioned her name. Your children with Brenda hold no blame. Brenda served a purpose. The gods are very pleased with the outcome. I do not hold any ill will towards her. She gave me the greatest gift I could ask for."

"You must come back to Skagen with me!" he said. "I cannot believe that you are still alive! You must meet your brothers and sisters!"

"No, father, it is not possible." she said. "My place is here in Kattegat. Idun sent you to me so that I may help you when you need it. Freki is strong. You must not worry about him. Aesir, Erika, Magna, and Kirsten will also be okay. They are smarter than you think."

She held out her left hand and he licked it. He reached in his pocket and pulled out a huge handful of gold pieces. She held up her hand.

"6 silver pieces is my price." she said.

"I want you to have it!" he said. "Please accept it!"

"I cannot." she said. "I know that you are a very rich man, yet I have rules to live by. I need not for money. Give me 6 silver pieces."

"I do not like it, but I cannot argue." he said. "I guess if you can survive in the wilderness for 26 years, you truly do *not* need for money."

He counted out 6 silver pieces.

"And father?" she said. "Nobody can know that I am alive."

"I suppose that is for the best." he said. "But I *will* be back to see you."

He turned and walked out of the tent. He was stunned. How could she have survived? She said that the wolves helped her, but he had never met a friendly wolf.

She was obviously in touch with the gods, and very close to them. He suspected that she got some help from them as well. But why? She was less than 5 years old at the time.

He had often wondered why the gods put Margaret in front of him. There was never any woman at any other time on that voyage except for Brenda, then on the last stop, she appeared. She said exactly what was required to get him to take her back with them. Did she have special powers? Did the gods touch her as well? Her daughter was blessed, and that didn't come from Gardi. The type of power that Disa has is something that you are *born* with.

Although Margaret was born in Wales, and lived in England, she had some mystic powers. Gardi realized this a week or two after they got back to Skagen. Things would appear in exactly the right place, and the right time that Margaret needed them. She was able to talk him into doing things that he had no intention of doing, with a smile and a wink. Things that Gardi would *never* be inclined to do on his own. Like sleep with her.

She seemed to know everything about the Norse gods immediately. She knew more that Gardi did, for that matter, she even knew more than *Astrid* ever did.

At the time he picked her up from Lindisfarne, he didn't have any ideas about sleeping with her. When he got back she slowly started working on him. With Astrid gone, and Brenda moody and occupied with her pregnancy, he eventually succumbed to her advances. They kept the secret well, until she became pregnant. Brenda hit the roof. He never admitted to it; he feared for Margaret's safety. Brenda knew though. Margaret tried to tell her that it was the stable boy, but Brenda didn't buy it.

After Disa was born, and Gardi was a little more distracted she disappeared within a few months. Margaret seldom left the house, but it was a beautiful spring morning and she wanted to get some air. She never returned. Gardi knew, but he didn't know. He couldn't prove anything. Baldur had been born, and Brenda was pregnant with Leif. After Margaret disappeared, Brenda was extra sweet. Gardi never brought it up, he figured that no good could come of it. Soon Leif was born, and Margaret faded from everyone's mind. A few years later, Disa disappeared.

He never let on, but He mourned Disa for a long time. Brenda focused on her kids, and tried to get Gardi to participate as much as possible. He loved Baldur and Leif, but he never stopped thinking about Disa. She was the first child of his that he lost.

And now she was back. He would love to talk to her some more about her life. He wanted to continue talking to her today, but when she held out her left hand, he knew it was over. He would come back down to Kattegat the following week and talk to her again.

He wished that she would invite him over socially, for dinner or something. How did she live? Did she have a good house? A husband? She had lived in the woods for 26 years, it probably took her quite a while to acquire social skills. Maybe not. She was very smart, and gifted with the second sight. Stronger than Astrid or Helga. Did she have friends? Children? He would find out one way or another.

He would ask Idun. If he was lucky, he might get an answer. Idun had set him up. She had to know that the seer was Disa. There must be a reason that she sent him.

Disa had assured him that Freki and his family would be okay. He felt a little better with both Idun and Disa agreeing on it. He felt powerless to do anything, since they were in England. He would make it a point to talk to him while they were over there.

He thought about Lagertha. Why was Idun so interested? She claimed that the other gods were interested as well. She was an excellent warrior, and smart too. Maybe that was it. She was a descendant of Odin, and that was important.

Maybe that was why Idun was always asking about her love life. They wanted her to have children. Gardi was doubtful that that would ever happen. Lagertha scared men away. Men were nowhere near as brave these days. A lot of men marveled at how Gardi was able to tame Brenda, but if she were available back then, she would have had plenty of takers. Today, nobody would want anything to do with her. Idun was right, the world was changing.

He pulled into the dock at Skagen and Lagertha greeted him.

"Hello daddy, where have you been?" she asked.

"I went to see a woman in Kattegat." he said.

"Really?" she asked. "What was it about?"

"I was sent there by Idun." he said. "I've been worried about Freki."

"Freki will be fine." she said. "He would be a lot better if he got rid of that bitch, but he can take care of himself."

"How do you know?" asked Gardi.

"Freki has 2 faces." she said. "The one he shows the world, and the one that he really is. He may appear to be under her control, and that might be what he wants people to see, but he's a different person inside. His mind is strong enough to resist her. He keeps up appearances for the children, but he's still one of us. So are the children."

"I admire your optimism." he said. "I hope you're right."

"I am." she said. "I would love to go over there and take care of her myself. Take her for a little 'walk in the forest' like mama used to do."

"Although your mother's walks in the forest were effective, they were not always the right thing." he said, thinking about Margaret. "You should stay away from that."

"I've never killed anyone who didn't deserve it, daddy." she said. "I don't think you have either. I never knew mama, but I understand her."

"You don't know how right you are." he said. "It's like your mind and body were taken over by her spirit the day she died."

"Is that a problem?" she asked.

"No, I'm grateful." he said. "It's like she's still here."

"Have you thought about what we discussed?" she asked.

"Your brothers are going to be pissed, but you have earned the honor." he said. "You will be the captain of one of my boats on the voyage."

She uncharacteristically squealed and did a little dance right there in the road.

"Careful." he said. "One of these men around here may mistake you for a maiden."

"Don't worry, I will put them in their place." she said. "Remember Gunnar?"

"I've been meaning to talk to you about that." he said. "Not Gunnar, but your whole attitude about men. I would like to have some grandchildren from you someday."

"Are you serious?" she asked. "You have a lot of grandchildren already. Do you think any of these pussies around here are up to the challenge?"

"I'm sure that they would be if you gave them a chance." he said. "You're a beautiful girl."

He was trying to nudge her in the direction that Idun wanted. He didn't know why she wanted that, but he wanted to help out. And he really *did* want grandchildren from her.

"I'll think about it, daddy." she said. "You're the expert, how is married life?"

"It's very rewarding." he said. "If your mother and I never married, you wouldn't be alive. Some important people would like to see you move in that direction."

"Really? Who?" she asked.

"I can't tell you." he said. "Just do me a favor, think about it?"

"Ok, daddy." she said. "It will have to be someone of my choosing."

"Although I am a powerful man, I would never presume to marry you off to someone for political or financial gain." he said. "If I did that, I might be the next one to 'take a walk in the forest'."

"Even if I wanted to, what good would that do me?" she said. "You have this annoying habit of not staying dead."

They both laughed.

"Just stay open to it." he said. "And stop being so mean to the men."

"I'm not mean, I'm just misunderstood." she said. "You don't think I would enjoy being normal? With a husband at home?"

"Say what you like, elsker, but you will never be normal." he said. "But I wouldn't change a thing. Let's start with finding a man first, and go from there."

"It may take some time, but I'll think about it." she said.

"That's all I ask." he said.

"Thank you for making me captain, daddy." she said. "I won't let you down."

"Now I have to sell it to your brothers." he said.

"Don't worry about Kol and Bjørn." she said. "They wouldn't dare object. What a happy coincidence that Gunhilda and Hjordís are both about to have a babies. Even if they *were* to protest, their wives would put them in their place. They probably want Kol and Bjørn to stay home and suffer with them."

"Take it from me. *That* would be a disaster." he said. "A Viking needs to raid. More marriages have been broken up from husbands staying home during pregnancies than going away."

"They can raid. I will too. I might even let one of them on my boat." she said with a wicked grin.

"That's my girl." he said.

She thought about her last trip to England, when they went to see Freki. She thought about Alfdis. She really *would* take her for a walk in the forest.

That bitch actually thought that she could convert her. She remembered it like it happened yesterday.

"Just give it a chance." she said. "He loves us all! He forgives our sins, no matter what they are."

"That's funny. As far as I'm concerned, I don't have any sins." she said.

"Oh, come now, Lagertha, You've killed people." she said. "But none of that matters! He died on the cross to forgive our sins! He gives this gift freely to all of us! It doesn't matter what you've done, if you accept him, you are forgiven."

"How is killing someone who deserves it wrong?" she asked. "And why would I worship a man who was such a weakling? If he was so powerful, why didn't he stop them? He even helped them! He carried the cross! So they could nail him to it and kill him!"

"But he rose again 3 days later!" she said. "Why don't you talk about that?"

They *said* he rose again." she said. "These men who made up the rest of it. How can you be so gullible?"

"The bible was written by God!" she said. "It was divinely inspired!"

"So your god came down to earth and wrote all of this down?" she asked. "I thought he was too busy making his son look like a coward."

"No, the Gospels were written by Matthew, Mark, Luke, and John." she said. "They were apostles of Jesus. They were there! They saw everything!"

"And they did nothing? What kind of friend is that?" she said. "I bet they made it all up to hide their own guilt for abandoning their friend. A Norseman would never do that!"

"How dare you compare Jesus Christ to Norsemen!" she asked. "There is no comparison."

"You got that right." she said. "No self-respecting Norseman would ever be such a pussy! How could you go from such strong gods to a weakling that can't even save himself from mortals?"

"He wasn't supposed to save himself!" she said. "He knew that he was going to die. He died to take away our sins. Please come with me to church! You will see."

Maybe you should come to *my* church." she said. "It's just up the path in the forest."

"You don't scare me." she said. "I am doing God's work. I will save you. Trust me."

She moved a little closer to Lagertha and tried to put her arm around her.

Lagertha grabbed her hand, twisted it around her back, and put her dagger to her throat.

Just then Gardi walked in.

"Let her go." he said.

"But daddy! You haven't heard how she's been talking!" she said. "She's trying to convert me to the false god!"

"She is your brother's wife." he said. "She's a little mixed up right now, but she's family. We don't kill family."

She loosened her grip and pushed her hard, sending her sprawling across the floor and into the table. She got up unsteady, and had a stream of blood rolling down her forehead.

Lagertha took a step towards her.

"THAT"S ENOUGH!" said Gardi.

"Fine." she said and walked out in a huff.

She better watch it this time around, she thought. If she's not careful, I *will* kill her. I'll do it at midnight, gagged and trussed if I have to.

Asgard

"How is the girl?" asked Thor.

"She is wonderful!" said Idun. "Gardi will make her a captain on the next voyage."

"Has she found a man yet?" asked Odin.

"Her personality does not encourage courting." she said. "Men are not as they used to be. 50 years ago, there would be plenty of candidates. Now…"

Remembering a past meeting, Loki looked at Freyja.

In his best little girl voice He shrieked "I volunteer!"

"Your stock is so weak, little brother, that it would be counterproductive." said Thor. "Try to be serious."

"Perhaps I could give her some pointers." said Freyja.

"*Nobody* is going down there!" shouted Odin. "This is something that she must change on her own."

"How much longer?" asked Thor.

"We have not even decided to do it." said Loki. "I for one am against it."

"Really?" said Thor. "You are against something that makes sense. I never would have thought."

"Quiet down, you two. Loki is right." said Odin. "We cannot make this decision lightly. If we had to decide today, I would also vote against it."

Loki smiled broadly and raised his middle finger to Thor.

"What else is going on, Idun?" he asked.

"He worries for Freki and his family." said Idun. "Alfdis has already converted."

"Do you see?" said Thor. "One of the weak wives produces a weak child."

"Do not underestimate Freki." said Idun. "He has inner strength."

"What is wrong with having some smart ones?" asked Loki. "Must they all be dumb and strong?"

Thor glared at him.

"It is wise to have descendants with diverse qualities." said Odin. "We are doing well with the warriors, as well as intellectuals. Do not forget that being smart does not mean that they cannot fight. Freki has proven that."

"He seems too squeamish to me." said Thor.

He may not be as exciting as the warriors, but brains can be sexy too!" said Freyja. "Your father is right. We need descendants from all walks of life."

"I cannot complain." said Thor. "He has produced many great warriors. Which is why we should go ahead with the plan."

"There is no plan." said Odin. "Just a crazy idea that I do not like."

"I defer to your wisdom, father." said Thor. "Promise me that you will think about it."

"I do not need to promise you anything." he said. "I am the father, and you are the son."

Loki started laughing.

"Shut up!" boomed Odin. "The fact that you are against this does not work in your favor. I will always think harder about things that *you* support. Idun, you will keep us abreast of any developments. That is all."

3

He was laying on his back looking at the stars. He found Nidhogg, Ratatosk, and Friggerock. The Eagle was between Nidhogg and Ratatosk. Closer to the horizon were The Eyes of Thjazi.

After 54 years, he knew her very well. He knew she was coming. She showed up moments later.

"Did you see the woman in Kattegat?" she asked.

"Yes. That was a cute trick you pulled on me." he said. "Any more surprises on the horizon?"

"I could not tell you who she was." she said. "That was up to her to divulge. Surely you understand?"

"Yes." he said. "But if she did not tell me, then I would not know that my daughter is alive. Was there a reason that you sent me to her?"

"She is a good seer." she said. "You seemed troubled. Did she help?"

"Yes, she agreed with you that Freki will be okay." he said. "You know that I have mourned her ever since she 'died'. I would have loved to have known she was alive long ago."

"Like I said, dear Gardi, it was not my place to reveal her." she said. "That was something that I had to leave up to her. What if she did not want to be found by you?"

"But she did…at least I *think* she did." he said, suddenly not sure.

"What makes you think that she did not?" she asked.

"I do not know." he said. "I guess that I expected her to be happier to see me."

"She has had a difficult life." she said, frowning. "It was quite an ordeal for her to merely survive. If you continue to see her, I promise that more will be revealed."

"Can you tell me anything about her?" he asked. "Is she married? Does she have children? Does she have a good life?"

"Again, sweet Gardi, those things are up to her to disclose." she said. "Will you see her again?"

"I plan a trip back down there next week." he said. "Hopefully it will not be all business."

"How is Lagertha?" she asked.

"She is well." he said. "I told her of my decision about making her captain."

"I am sure she was proud!" she said. "You have some more grandchildren on the way. How are Gunhilda and Hjordís?"

"They are at the point where they only want it to be over. According to Baldur, I may be a great grandfather soon." he said.

"Really?" she asked. "Which one?"

"Brenda." he said. "They are not sure yet, but she is convinced. I spoke to Lagertha about maybe getting married and having one of her own."

"And how did she respond to that?" she asked.

"About as you would expect." he asked. "But she promised to give it some thought."

"She has to start somewhere." said Idun. "I just think she is such a lovely girl, and it would be a shame if she didn't."

Gardi started laughing.

"Lovely girl?" he asked. "Do you not remember her mother? Lagertha is just the same. The only possible difference is that she may actually be meaner than Brenda. She may need to change more than she would like to if she has any hope of finding a man."

"Keep encouraging her, dear Gardi." she said. "If you have not figured it out yet, Lagertha is very important. We want her to be happy."

"Why is she so important?" he asked.

"Because the gods have taken an interest in her." she said. "When you go to see Disa again, ask her about her mother. She may be able to give you some peace. I must go now, Gardi. We will speak again soon."

She took a little hop off the ground and left a luminescent trail to the heavens.

* * *

"Why won't you go?" she asked.

"It's just not my thing." said Freki. "I've never been religious. I went last week. You go. I don't mind at all."

"But it's *my* thing, which means it should be yours!" said Alfdis. "I want the children to start coming too. I worry about your soul!"

"Eight years ago you didn't even know what a soul was." he said. "All of the kids are old enough to make up their own minds on this, except for Kirsten. And so am I."

"You are a smart man, Freki, all you need to do is listen to know the truth." she said.

"Are you forgetting who my father is?" he asked.

He had participated in this discussion too many times. He had told her repeatedly that he didn't mind if she went. What he said was true; he really *wasn't* religious.

He had personally come to doubt that there was any higher power at all. He believed in the Norse gods for most of his life, then he went to church with her. Listening to the priest, and the talk of Jesus somehow made him doubt everything. It all sounded like fairy stories to him, which also made him doubt the Norse gods. Neither seemed believable to him. His father's immortality didn't even sway him much. There was so much that was unknown about the human condition.

He had begun to study science in secret after they moved to England. He learned to read, and met frequently with a man named Henry Clark. He kept it a secret from Alfdis, because much of what he studied conflicted with her new beliefs.

He was willing to let her have her church, her Christianity, whatever she wanted. He even went with her occasionally, and pretended to be interested. He just could not believe as she did.

He had told Henry about his father. Henry figured that it was some type of medical anomaly. Freki tended to agree.

"I just fear for your immortal soul." she said. "Please come with me!"

He had an inward chuckle at her use of the word immortal. He sighed. He decided to go, if for no other reason than to keep the peace.

"Okay, I'll come with you this time." he said.

She looked him over skeptically.

"Is that what you're wearing?" she asked.

* * *

Baldur was walking through the forest. He was about to become a grandfather. His daughter Brenda, who he had named after his mother, was pregnant. Vali had confirmed it. He was happy of course, but it meant that he was officially becoming an old man. His sons, Kare and Dreng were both Vikings, and had never married. Brenda was a shield maiden, and would almost certainly go back to it after the child was born.

He thought about Freki. He wondered if any of his kids had children yet. Maybe he wasn't the first grandfather of this batch of Gardi's children. Freki was only a few months older than him, but he had always seemed more mature. Sure, Baldur had mellowed a bit over the years, but Freki was always more grown up, even when they were little.

For all the grief he gave Freki when they were younger, he had always respected him. It wasn't hard to figure out that he was smarter, that was apparent at an early age. And he *did* know how to fight, he just didn't enjoy it.

Gardi said it was because of his mother. Baldur had never met Astrid, but his father told him all about her.

From what he could tell, she was a lot like Ama, and of course, Brunhilda was a lot like Brenda. He wondered if Gardi had planned it that way. *Baldur* would have loved to have 2 wives that were opposites like that. Maybe when he was younger. Of course his father was still 28, and would be forever. Baldur was 54.

"*DUCK!*" she screamed.

Baldur instinctively fell to the ground. An arrow screamed through the air above his head and plunked into an 8 foot brown bear's chest as it let out a loud roar. He hadn't even seen the bear, he was so lost in his thoughts. Another arrow hit the bear, then Lagertha jumped over him, sword in hand. The bear was furious. She swung the sword at his neck as he raised a mighty paw to block it. Most of his forearm came clean off and flew 5 feet in the other direction. Lagertha thrust her sword into his chest with all her might, but this only made the animal angrier. She pulled the sword out and swung for his neck again. The bear tried to block the sword, but had apparently forgotten that he no longer had an arm. This one connected, and a fountain of blood started gushing from his neck. She had hit an artery. The bear was still pissed, but he was fading fast. He tried to roar at her again, but all that came out was a hoarse whisper. He turned to his right, then to his left, then he did an entire circle in place before falling to the ground with a loud thud.

"Are you following me?" he asked.

"I wasn't." she said. "But you got between me and my bear. You should be more careful, big brother."

"I was lost in thought." he said. "About Brenda…and Freki…well, lots of things."

"You should do your thinking in the privacy of your own home." she said. "You know how many people get hurt walking in the forest."

They both laughed. Brenda's exploits were a running joke.

"You are going to be an aunt." he said. "Vali confirmed it this morning."

"I already knew." she said. "I had a dream about it last week."

"Let's walk and talk." she said. "I need to go back up the path for Modi so I can haul this beast back."

"Pop told me about the voyage, congratulations." he said.

"Thank you." she said. "Can you give me some advice…about something else?"

"Sure, anything, sis." he said.

"Well, daddy thinks I should try to find a man." she said. "I'm thinking about doing it. What do men want?"

"For starters, they probably want to know that you won't kill them." he said. "Why the sudden interest?"

"He said that some important people are interested in seeing it happen." she said. "Think about it. Why would any of his political buddies give a shit?"

"I can't think of a reason." he said.

"And what other important people does daddy know?" she asked.

"He knows a lot of people." he said.

He knew what she was thinking.

"You don't really think…?" he asked.

"Why not?" she said. "It's not out of the realm of possibility. What else could he be talking about?"

"Do you think that his political buddies don't care, but somehow *they* do? The gods?" he asked.

"I asked him who, and he said that he couldn't say." she quipped.

"It could be anything, Lagertha." he said. "I doubt if it's the gods."

"All the same, I think I might try to do it." she said. "What do I have to lose?"

"I don't know, maybe a husband." he said.

"But I don't *have* a husband." she said. "So if I try it, and he turns out to be an asshole, it's no loss."

"I guess that's one way to look at it." he said.

"He was talking about children." she said. "He wants *me* to have children."

"Maybe he just wants more grandchildren." he said. "You know…from all his kids."

"So any advice?" she asked.

"Your looks have never been the problem." he asked. "Maybe you should try to tone down the aggression a little."

"I thought that men liked aggressive women." she said.

Maybe a little more Ama, and a little less Brunhilda." he said.

"Do I have to act like that little twit?!" she cried. "I can't do it."

"Not completely, but act a little less like a man." he said.

"I think I understand." she said.

"Don't get me wrong." he said. "Most guys like a little fire. They just want to be in control."

"Thanks, bro." she said.

They were back at the clearing where Modi was waiting. She gave him an apple. The horse gulped it down in one bite.

"Come on, big boy." she said. "It's time to go to work."

* * *

He entered the tent as she was lighting some incense.

"I knew you would be back." she said.

"If this is the only way I can see you, I'll be down often." he said. "I never stopped mourning you."

"I would have thought with all of your obligations that you would have forgotten me long ago." she said.

"If your child disappeared in her 4th year, could you forget?" he asked.

"I have never forgotten a thing in my life, father." she said.

"Really?" he asked. "How does that work?"

"You are not the only one who has been blessed by the gods." she said.

"So you have complete memory of *everything*?" he asked.

"Amongst other abilities." she said. "Did Idun send you?"

"Yes." he said. "She told me to ask you about your mother. She said maybe you can give me some peace."

"My mother is Danu." she said. "She is also Margaret's mother. We are Tuatha. She told you that she was from Wales. That is not entirely true. There is a land to the west known as Eire inhabited by the Celts. She grew up there. The Celtic people worship the same gods as you do, and many more. We use different names. You will find as you go on that many cultures worship the same gods. Danu is the goddess of magic and wisdom among other things. She is the one who helped me to survive in the forest for 26 years. She summoned Flidais, the goddess of the forest, woodlands, and wild things to charm the wolves into helping me."

So that's how she caught on to the Norse gods so quickly, he thought.

"So you are a descendant of a goddess?" he asked.

"Not a Norse goddess, but a powerful goddess nonetheless." she said. "Margaret is her daughter also. She knew who you were long before you met her in Lindisfarne. She was expecting you. As you were destined to be immortal, I was destined to become who I am. She knew that to fulfill this destiny, she had to have a child with you."

"So she knew what was going to happen all along?" he asked bewildered.

"We have a much stronger second sight than anything you have ever been exposed to." she said. "Not only that, we also see the past. Time is not linear for us. Margaret still exists, just not in this time. She knew what Brenda was going to do. She saw it before it happened, yet she knew it had to happen. Do you really think that she just decided one day that she 'needed some air', and walked into the forest?"

"Did she suffer?" he asked.

"I'm sure that while it was going on, she was somewhere else…or more specifically *sometime* else." she said. "She is far too powerful to ever let Brenda hurt her."

He couldn't believe what he was hearing. It was starting to make sense, though. He had always suspected that there was something different about Margaret. She had planned it all along. Maybe she knew for thousands of years the way Idun knew he was to be immortal. If Gardi was understanding it right, the descendants of Danu could put themselves in any place in time at will. *Time is not linear for us.*

"Is this why Idun sent me to you? I mean…besides the fact that you're my daughter that I haven't seen in 48 years?" he asked.

"We call her Armid." she said. "Time will become very important to you, father. Look at me as a guide."

"Why did she wait so long, Disa?" he said. "I guarantee that I would have wanted to know that you were alive."

"I also had a path to take." she said. "Had I not taken that path, I would not be here today. I would not have been able to help you. I would not be the same person. I would exist as someone else's son or daughter. Time is very delicate. A small ripple or breeze can change the world. Have you not seen the changes that are blowing in the wind?"

"I have." he said quietly.

"I am grateful that we have reconnected." she said.

She held out her left hand.

He wanted to know so much more, but he knew that it was over for today.

He licked her hand and counted out six silver pieces.

"I will be back soon." he said.

"I know that you will, father." she said.

4

She was in a strange land. There was a trial going on, and a long haired peaceful looking man was the defendant. The people were adamant that he was guilty. The crowd was loud and unruly, and they were shouting "Crucify him!"

From what she could understand, they were accusing him of corrupting the nation, not giving tribute to Caesar, and proclaiming himself Christ the King. The judge, who she had heard them call Pilate, seemed to be reluctant to punish him. He asked that they judge him by their own law. The leaders claimed that it was unlawful for them to put any man to death.

"Are you the King of the Jews?" asked Pilate.

"Do you not say that I am?" he asked.

"I am not a Jew." he replied. "Yet your own high priests have brought you to me. Why?"

"My kingdom is not of this world." was all he said.

"Are you a king?" he asked.

"You say that I am." he said. "I am here to testify the truth."

"And what is the truth?" he asked.

He remained silent.

The high priests questioned him and made accusations, yet still he said nothing.

"Do you not hear what they are accusing you of?" asked Pilate. "Have you nothing to say?"

He remained silent.

"I find him guilty of nothing." said Pilate.

The high priests protested that he had been teaching and creating havoc from Galilee to Jerusalem.

"Is he from Galilee?" asked Pilate.

They told him that he was.

Then I shall send him to Herod." he said. "This man Jesus is from Herod's jurisdiction, and it is his problem."

Suddenly she was in a different place, a lavish palace. There was an incredibly fat man questioning Jesus now. He questioned him at length, asking him numerous times to perform a miracle. Jesus said nothing. The high priests and scribes pleaded their case, to no avail. Herod and his soldiers mocked him and sent him back to Pilate.

"You have accused this man of corrupting the people, yet I have examined him and have found no guilt." said Pilate. "I may release one prisoner today for Passover. I have this man, and I have a murderer and thief named Barabbas. Which prisoner shall I release?"

The crowd enthusiastically shouted for him to release Barabbas and crucify Jesus.

Pilate went to a bowl of water and washed his hands.

"I wash my hands of the blood of this man." he said.

The high priests told him that his blood would be on their hands, and the hands of their children for eternity.

Now she was on the battlefield. There was a beautiful woman who was fighting 3 Christians. She had long black hair with a slight tinge of grey around the edges, and a black leather vest with a picture of a huge red dog on the back of it. She had lopped off one of the Christian's legs at the knee, and another's arm at the shoulder. She had a sword in one hand and the severed arm in the other. She was beating one of them in the head with the arm, while slashing the other's chest with her sword. She had a wild grin on her face. Suddenly an arrow pierced her chest, followed swiftly by 2 more. She fell to the ground clutching her chest. She heard a scream, and recognized the voice immediately. *"NO! NO! NO!!"* he shouted.

She saw Gardi running towards the woman.

"Daddy?!" she said.

He didn't hear her. He acted as if she wasn't there at all.

"DADDY! I'M OVER HERE!" she screamed.

"*NO!!*" he cried. "*NO! NOT HER! ANYONE BUT HER!*"

He cradled her in his arms and was mumbling sweetly to her.

Suddenly she was in the sky. She was not floating, she was inside an impossibly tall building. She looked through a strange, hard, clear barrier and saw several small bugs of different colors busily speeding around in trenches that they had dug in the ground.

A woman was sitting in front of a small table with a large board in front of her, which had words and pictures on the side that was facing her. She was dressed very strangely. Suddenly a loud ringing sound broke the silence. The woman picked up a small object and brought it to her ear.

"Mr. Singer's office, how may I help you?" she said. Lagertha couldn't understand what was going on. The woman continued to speak into the device, then put it back in its cradle. A man walked into the room.

"I need those reports on my desk by noon, Marsha." he said. "And when you have a minute, could you bring me some coffee?"

"Yes, Mr. Singer, right away." she replied.

The woman went into an attached room and picked up a small clear vessel, then went to a small silver trench and turned a knob above it. To Lagertha's surprise, water started gushing from a long silver tube just above the trench. The woman filled the clear vessel, then turned the knob again, and the water stopped flowing instantly. She put some finely ground dark brown dirt into a cup, then slid the cup into a slot attached to a very strange device. She poured the water into the top of the device, then put the vessel beneath it. Brown water came out filling up the vessel. It smelled good, not like dirt at all.

She looked up and saw the biggest bird she had ever seen in her life heading straight for the building. The bird had 3 stripes on it, and it was the color of a silver coin. It had no feathers, and its wingspan was at least 50 yards wide. How does this bird not see the building? Just as it was about to hit the building, she woke up.

* * *

"I had a very strange dream last night, daddy." she said. "First there was a man who was on trial. There was a huge mob calling for his death. He did nothing to defend himself, it was almost as if he wanted to die. The judge offered to let one of the prisoners go, this man, or another named Barabbas who was a murderer. They screamed to let the murderer go and crucify the other one. Then I was on the battlefield, and there was a beautiful woman in a vest with a large red dog on the back of it."

Gardi perked up at this.

"She was fighting 3 Christians, and doing pretty good. Then 3 arrows hit her, and she fell to the ground dead. Then *you* ran to her. I tried to get your attention, but it was as if I wasn't there. You didn't hear me at all. Next I was inside of a building that reached the clouds. The people were dressed very strangely. A strange bird that was as big as Yggdrasil flew straight at me. I woke up before the bird got there."

It all came back to him. She described Brenda's death perfectly, as if she was there and witnessed it herself. Brenda had a vest made after Zeke died with a picture of him on the back. She really loved that dog. She wore the vest into battle every time she fought. She was wearing it the day that she died...and it was 3 arrows that killed her.

He thought about what Disa had said about moving around in time. It was as though Lagertha was there at the scene when Brenda died. She told the story perfectly. The trial she described sounded like what he had heard from Alfdis about the false god. He was certain that Lagertha had never heard this tale. He didn't know what to make of the tall building and the gigantic bird. Perhaps it was from the future. Gardi had never seen a building that was more than 2 stories tall.

"Tell me more about the woman, the warrior." he said.

"She had cut off one of their legs at the knee, and another's arm. She was beating one of them with the arm when she was shot." she said. "You could tell that she knew what she was doing."

"Does it mean anything to you, daddy?" she asked. "I mean...you were there."

There was no way she could have known any of this. She was barely a year old at the time. He had only told her that Brenda died in battle, but with the details of her dream, there could be no mistake. Brenda died with a severed left arm in her hand.

I-I don't know how to tell you this honey, it is a little scary." he said.

This was the first time that she had ever seen her father at a loss for words, and he *did* seem a little scared.

"Daddy?!" she said.

"You just described perfectly the day that your mother died."

Was it possible that she had the same ability as Disa? Is that why the gods were so interested? It couldn't be, he thought. She only knew the Norse gods. It was just a dream. An incredibly accurate dream. Astrid's words came back to him. *There is no such thing as 'just a dream'.*

He would talk to Idun tonight, then head back down to Kattegat to talk to Disa. What was happening with his little girl?

* * *

The priest was telling the story of how Jesus had raised Lazarus from the dead. Freki pretended to listen and be interested, but he did not believe.

He had discussed this tale with Henry, and they concluded that Lazarus was never dead in the first place. He was in a coma. Jesus was fortunate enough to approach him at the same time that he awoke. That is, if it ever happened at all. The Christians relied solely on the word of people who lived hundreds of years ago, and took everything they heard as the truth, without question.

Freki couldn't understand how *anyone* could so blindly believe these stories simply because someone had written them down. Did they think that these men were incapable of lying? Alfdis said that it was faith that made people believe. He needed something more solid than wishful thinking. He needed proof.

He felt the same way about the 'resurrection'. He figured that Jesus had taken some kind of potion that made him appear to be dead for 3 days, then miraculously 'rose from the dead' to make the story more believable. It upset him to see Alfdis swallow these lies without a second thought. She was a smart woman, but she could be gullible.

He felt a sharp kick on his leg. He looked down and Alfdis was glaring at him. He looked back up at the priest. He didn't understand what the problem was. He had told her numerous times that he didn't want to go to church. Did he force her to come along when he was doing *his* things? She had become increasingly demanding about him going to church lately. Could he just put his foot down and refuse to go? Would there ever be peace in his household if he did?

Thinking about it, he had to admit that he was not at peace right now. They would have to have a serious conversation on the subject with her soon.

They had grown apart, and it was all due to her new religion. He wasn't even sure that he wanted to be married to her anymore. The children were all grown up with the exception of Kirsten who was 7 years old. Would she be able to handle it if they split? He thought so. She was very mature, and incredibly smart. He figured that she already knew about the problems.

He looked down at her. She was very attentive to the priest, and looked the part to her mother. She never let on, but she was always asking Freki about the Norse gods. She was very curious, he knew that she got that from him.

He kept his atheist views to himself. He didn't want to confuse her, and he figured that she should grow up believing in *something*. He had no doubt that she would figure it out for herself when the time came.

* * *

He was looking at the stars. He recognized all of the Norse constellations, and lately had been trying to find new ones of his own. If he looked hard enough, he could connect enough stars to make almost anything. Of course none of his creations were anywhere near as spectacular as the *real* ones, but it was fun.

"Gazing at the stars again?" she asked.

He got up and dusted himself off.

"I like to try to find new constellations." he said. "We need to talk."

"What is it, elsker?" asked Idun.

"It is my daughter. You know? Our special girl." he said. "She had a disturbing dream."

"And what was it about?" she asked.

"It was about the death of her mother." he said. "And the crucifying of the false god. She also was in a building that reached the clouds, and she saw a giant bird."

"And what does this dream mean to you, sweet Gardi?" she asked.

"She described in perfect detail Brenda's death, right down to what she was wearing." he said. "Do you know a goddess named Danu?"

"Yes, I am familiar with Danu." she said. "How do you know about her?"

Was it happening already? Did she go behind our backs? We didn't even agree to our part.

"I think you know very well." he said. "Did you not tell me to ask Disa about her mother?"

"So you think that Lagertha is travelling through time?" she asked.

"Does it not seem that way to you?" he asked. "Have you ever seen a building that reaches the clouds? How would she know about the trial of Jesus? And it was like she was there on the battlefield for her mother's death."

"Dear Gardi, it was only a dream." she said.

"I think you know that there is no such thing as 'only a dream'." he said. "She knows details that no one could know if they were not there."

"I must speak to the other gods." she said. "You will meet me here tomorrow at dusk."

"What is going on?" he asked. "Why must you speak to the others?"

"I cannot tell you right now." she said. "All will be revealed tomorrow. And Gardi?"

He looked up.

"Yes?" he asked.

"Bring Lagertha." she said.

With that she was off into the night sky, leaving Gardi to wonder why.

5

Asgard

"Did she go behind our backs?" asked Odin.

"Not exactly, she has only walked in her dreams." said Idun. "I asked her to come today, but I told her that it was at 6:15 so that we would have time to talk."

"I had not made a decision on this, but it appears that she is forcing my hand." said Odin. "We cannot make Lagertha immortal. There can be only one."

"The other option is still available." she said.

"I never had any illusions that she would be immortal." said Thor. "I can live with the other option, as long as she takes care of herself."

"How soon you forget who we are talking about, big brother." said Loki. "Will *you* be the one who tells her that she must be careful?"

"Remember what father said the last time. We are forbidden to intervene." he said. "That task will fall on her father."

"You will make sure that Gardi understands this, Idun?" asked Odin.

"He will know." she said. "I do not anticipate any problems."

"So…how will this work?" asked Freyja. "She will be able to walk as her half-sister does?"

"Yes, but she will have obvious advantages over Disa." said Odin. "For one, she will not scare people away."

"Do *you* forget of whom we talk, father?" asked Loki.

"I think that you know what I mean, Loki." he said. "Her appearance is much more pleasant."

"You can say that again!" squealed Freyja.

"Are you prepared, Idun?" asked Odin.

"Everything is ready." she said. "I told Gardi to bring her along tonight."

"A bit presumptuous, is it not?" he said, glaring at her.

"I do not think so." she said. "You have heard the dreams. If we allow Danu to proceed without us, we will lose control."

He sighed.

"Of course you are right." he said. "I am not used to being second guessed, even by the most powerful Celtic goddess, who is technically my mother. I will allow it, but only what we talked about before."

Just then Heimdallr walked in.

"Pardon the intrusion, father." he said. "Danu is here."

"She's early." he said. "Send her in."

* * *

"Where are we going, daddy?" she asked.

He didn't know how to tell her. *He* didn't even know why she was tagging along. He didn't have a choice. Idun told him to bring her. Then flew away before he could protest, or ask any questions. He guessed that he should just tell her, so she could be prepared.

"Remember those important people I was talking about? The ones who are interested in your love life?" he asked.

"Of course, daddy." she said.

"We are meeting with one of them." he said.

He tried to think of a diplomatic way to tell her the rest, but he couldn't come up with anything. The sun was low on the horizon, setting over the North Sea. Whether he told her or not was irrelevant, Idun was never late.

"Who, daddy?" she asked.

He sighed. He couldn't complain, it was nowhere near the hardest thing Idun had ever asked him to do.

"She will be here soon enough." he said. "She is an important counsel to me."

Could it be? Was she going to meet one of the gods?

The last sliver of the sun sank below the water.

"Greetings, sweet Gardi, and the Lagertha, elsker." she said.

She was illuminated as she was the first time that they met after dark. The edges of her white robe glowed, as did her blond hair. Her blue eyes shined as though they had candles behind them.

Lagertha was stunned. Her jaw dropped. She fell to her knees and bowed her head.

"I suppose that we must go over this again." she said. "Rise dear Lagertha, we will not stand on ceremony among friends."

She slowly lifted her head and looked at Idun, then at Gardi.

"You better do as she says." he said.

She slowly rose to her feet.

"But...why?" she asked. "Why me?"

"Yes, I was wondering about that *myself*." said Gardi.

"The gods have taken an interest in you from an early age." she said. "Do you remember the dream that you had a few nights ago?"

"Of course. After daddy told me that it was about mama, I could hardly think about anything else." she said. "And those other strange things."

"You were travelling through time in your dream, elsker." she said. "Would you like to be able to do that in your waking life?"

"I do not know." she said.

"There is an old goddess. Her name is Danu." she said. "She is not a Norse goddess. She is Celtic goddess from a land known as Eire across the sea. We have been working together for thousands of years. She too has shown an interest in you. She would like to teach you how to walk through time."

"I will ask you again, why me?" she said.

Like Gardi, Lagertha immediately regretted questioning Idun.

Idun raised an eyebrow.

"Why not you?" she asked.

"I-I do not know." she said. "This is all very sudden."

"I have a gift for you." she said.

She reached into the air, and a cup of water materialized in her hand.

"This is not the same as the gift that I gave your father." she said. "You will not become immortal. There can be only one, and that one is your father. You must be careful not to die. This water is from the fountain of youth, and will stop the aging process within you. It is a gift from the Norse gods, whether you decide to work with Danu or not. You will never get any older than you are now. You will be young and beautiful for eternity!"

She reached out and took the cup.

"Odin would like it very much if you learn from Danu, but it is not required." she said. "The water of youth is a gift to you with no obligations."

She looked at Idun, then at Gardi, then at the cup. Her hand was shaking. The water was a mystical blue, with light green foam circling the cup.

"You must drink it, dear." said Idun.

Gardi shrugged his shoulders.

"I have learned a long time ago not to argue with her, but this must be your decision. It is something you must live with. This is a surprise to me as well, she did not tell me." he said, giving Idun a stern look. "I have never known her to be wrong. I suggest that you drink the water."

"Okay, daddy." she said.

She took a sip. It tasted sweet, but not too sweet. It was the perfect combination of sweet and tart. She felt a sudden surge of energy. She felt more alive than she ever had before. She took another tentative sip, then gulped down the rest.

"Is there more?" she asked.

"What you have consumed is a potent dose." said Idun, frowning. "It will last you hundreds of years. If it should become necessary, you will get more. I know how lovely it tastes, but there can be too much of a good thing."

"So what happens next?" she asked.

"You will have to decide whether you would like to work with Danu or not." said Idun. "I think that you already know what you will do."

"Really?" she asked. "Perhaps you would like to enlighten me."

"You are a proactive person, dear Lagertha." she said. "I know that you would not want to disappoint the gods. Think of the things you could do if you have this power."

"So I will never get old?" she asked.

"No elsker, but it is important to remember that you will not be immortal." she said. "You are of great importance. Care must be taken that you do not die."

"I am not a cautious person." she said. "I do not know how to be careful. I only know how to fight as I always have."

"You are your father's daughter." she said. "He also knows no other way. Danu can certainly help you with that."

"A goddess? Teaching me how to fight?" she asked.

"It will be more of a lesson in how to stay alive." she said. "When you are ready, you will come to the forest and find a secluded spot like this, and she will find you."

"Okay." she said quietly. "I will do as you ask."

"For the moment, this must be a secret between the three of us." she said. "You must not tell anyone else about this."

"I will not." she said.

"There is a seer in Kattegat that can help you." she said. "She works near the docks. You will wait until after you meet with Danu to see her."

Gardi was shocked. She was sending her to Disa? The girl who her mother maimed? Her half-sister? Was this really necessary? Disa had told him that no one else could know that she was still alive. Did she know that Lagertha would be coming? Of course she would know, she knew everything it seemed. He wasn't sure how he felt about this.

Idun could see that Gardi was troubled.

"I think that your father would like to talk to me alone." she said. "Would you be so kind as to take a short nap?"

"Of course." she said.

Lagertha curled up next to the tree and was snoring softly moments later.

"So why are you sending her to Disa?" he asked. "She told me that nobody can know that she is still alive."

"And nobody will." said Idun. "She was 26 years old when Lagertha was born. Lagertha does not know about her. Disa will not say anything. What are you worried about, Gardi?"

"I just think that it is creepy that she will be consulting with her half-sister, who she doesn't even know exists." he said. "I have only recently discovered that she is alive, and I never thought that my daughter would meet her, especially under such dubious circumstances."

She gave him a puzzled look.

"I doubt that you ever expected that she would meet me either, yet here we are." she said.

"But this is different." he said. "Disa is her *sister*!"

"Nevertheless, you must admit that Disa will have valuable information for her." she said. "She has lived this life for a half century. Lagertha needs guidance."

"You always know best." he said. "I guess I must keep the secret as well."

"You must also make sure that she is careful." she said. "At least until she has learned from Danu. How soon do you sail?"

"In less than a month." he said.

"Rise, dear Lagertha." she said.

Lagertha shook her head for a second and was wide awake.

"I would like for you to find a man." she said. "One of your father's directives is to create descendants of Odin. That will be your task as well."

"It will have to be a man of my choosing." she said. "I will do as you ask, but it may take some time."

"When you become receptive to the idea, you will be amazed with the results!" she said. "Sweet Lagertha, I must also caution you to meet with Danu as soon as possible. You must give yourself some time with her before the voyage. She will help you. You must meet with her before going into battle."

"I will." she said.

There was a rustling in the weeds to the west. Lagertha looked in that direction, and Idun was gone.

* * *

He was sitting by the river fishing. A man wearing a long white robe came out of the forest and sat down next to him. He had long hair and a beard. He reminded Freki of the Vikings back home, except that this man seemed so peaceful.

"Catching anything?" he asked.

"Not a nibble all day." he said.

Perhaps you are using the wrong bait." he said.

He reached into his pocket and pulled out a small wafer.

"Try this." he said.

It looked like the wafers he had seen at mass with Alfdis that were supposed to represent the body of Christ. The words of the priest echoed in his head *Corpus Christi*. Going to mass wasn't a complete waste of time, he was starting to pick up some Latin.

"Go ahead!" he cried. "Give it a try! It never fails!"

Freki pulled his line in and took the wafer. He examined it closely. It had a perfect impression of a cross on it. It was definitely one of the wafers from the church. The man said it worked every time, and Freki was hungry. It couldn't be sacrilegious if he didn't believe, could it?

"Are you sure?" he asked. "You know what this is, don't you?"

"Yes, I have been catching people with it for years!" he said. "Once you try it, you will never go back!"

People?

"You mean fish, right?" he asked.

"What did I say?" he asked. "Did I say people? Merely a slip of the tongue. Of course I meant fish."

He looked at the wafer again. It didn't seem right, he knew that this was from the church, and he didn't want to show any disrespect, even though he *did* think it was all a fairy tale.

The man looked at him nervously. It was as if Freki putting the wafer on the hook was extremely important.

"Are you not going to try it?" he asked.

"You know that I don't believe, right?" he asked.

"That is why we call it faith, Freki." he said. "You must take the first step."

"How do you know my name?" he asked.

"Oh, I know all about you." he said. "Why do you think that I joined you here today?"

"I hope that you're not trying to convert me, because if you are, you're wasting your time." he said. "I need proof."

"Look around you." he said. "You see the river, the trees, and the birds singing. Who do you think created all of this?"

Freki scoffed.

"It can all be explained by science." he said.

"But can science explain how *all of this* was created?" he asked.

"Not completely, but many scientists have theories." he said.

"And who created those scientists?" he asked. "I thought that you needed proof."

"Their mothers and fathers, of course." he said.

"We are all descendants of Adam and Eve." he said. "And God created them…as well as everything you see around you."

"That's a nice story, but there is no proof." he said. "There are only a bunch of men who wrote stories hundreds of years ago. Am I to take their fantasies as reality?"

The man shrugged his shoulders.

"That is for you to decide." he said. "Are you going to try my bait or not? I promise that you will catch something."

"And what if I don't?" he asked.

"Then you will be no worse off than you were before." he said. "You *must* take the first step, Freki."

What did he have to lose? He baited the hook with the wafer and tossed it into the water.

Almost immediately he felt a sharp tug on the line. He pulled with all of his might, but made little progress.

"I told you!" said the man excitedly. "It looks like a big one."

Freki kept pulling, wrapping the line around the pole when it slacked. Finally it broke the water, and with a powerful pull, he brought it onto the riverbank.

He looked down in horror. It was Alfdis. She was flopping around like a fish.

"Thank you, Freki!" she said. "You saved me! Now you must be saved!"

"But I do not want to be saved!" he said.

She looked at him shocked. Why didn't he want to be saved?

The man started laughing loudly.

"I told you it would work!" he said. "I hooked *her* with the same bait! Now come with me and be a fisher of men!"

He woke with a jolt.

It was only a dream. Gardi had told him that his mother used to say that there was no such thing as 'only a dream'.

6

She was in her element. It was always like this when she was fighting. She went into another world, another consciousness.

Arve was a huge man, he was 6'6" and 290 pounds of pure muscle. His blond hair went halfway down his back, and he had a neatly trimmed red beard.

Lagertha wasn't exactly small, like her mother, she was 6'1", and mean enough to scare most men. She wasn't scared of anything.

They were pacing in a circular motion, swords drawn and shields up, each waiting for the other to blink. There was a crowd of Vikings surrounding them urging them on.

"What's the matter, princess?" he asked. "Are you scared?"

"I think we both know better than that." she said through clinched teeth. "Are you? Scared?"

A chorus of laughter rang out from the spectators.

"A little." he said with a chuckle. "I'd be a fool not to be."

She took a swipe at his head, and he blocked it easily and countered with a jab to her ribs. He opened up a 3 inch gash between her bottom 2 ribs.

Now she was pissed. She didn't feel the pain. She never did. She was angry that he had cut her, and silently cursed herself for letting him do it.

She swung her shield at him, cutting his arm deeply between the elbow and shoulder.

He should have known better. He knew that she had some steel on her shield, all of Gardi's children did.

"How's that arm?" she asked.

"It's fine." he said. "How about those ribs?"

"What ribs?" she asked. "Did you get me?"

He lunged at her with his shield, aiming for her head, but she ducked out of the way. His sword hand was parallel with his shoulder, and she seized the opportunity to plunge her sword into the right side of his belly. He stumbled and fell onto his back. She quickly discarded her sword and shield and pounced on top of him. She reached behind her back, grabbed a dagger from her belt, and put it to his throat.

"Do you think it's funny now?!" she asked.

He raised his hand in protest just as she began cutting.

"*THAT"S ENOUGH!*" roared Gardi.

Her hand froze as a trickle of blood started running down his neck.

"*GET OFF OF HIM!*" yelled Gardi.

She spit in his face and begrudgingly stood up.

"There will be enough of us dying on the raids without us killing each other." he said. "I admire the enthusiasm, but save it for the Christi...I mean the...enemy."

"Lagertha! Go get Vali!" he said.

"I'm sorry, daddy, he just made me *so mad!*" she said.

"This man is your brother in arms!" he said. "He may save your life someday! Now go. Get your brother."

"Yes, father." she said.

She had her mother's temper, and it didn't take much to set her off.

Now they would be the same age forever...or at least as long as she lived. He didn't worry too much; if any of his children could take care of herself, it was Lagertha. Or Disa. She had lived through much more than *anyone* could expect.

"Are you going to live, Arve?" he asked.

"Remind me never to piss your daughter off!" he said. "I'll be fine as soon as Vali patches me up."

"Lagertha tears them apart, then Vali puts them back together again." he said.

They both laughed. Arve grabbed his gut in pain.

"Do me a favor?" he asked. "Don't make me laugh."

This only got them both laughing again.

They would be leaving in a few weeks, and Gardi was happy with the crew. He was looking forward to getting back out there. He looked forward to checking in on Freki.

He felt a little better after talking to Idun and Disa, but he couldn't help worrying. He needed to get back down to Kattegat and talk to Disa. He wanted to know more about what was happening with Lagertha. He was hopeful that he could get some answers. Both Idun and Disa had a habit of revealing as little as possible.

* * *

"Maybe it's nothing." she said. "But I saw her talking to him, and she was being *very* friendly."

"Oh?" said Brunhilda. "Why do you say that?"

It wasn't the first time that Ama had set Brunhilda up to fight one of her battles. She knew that Gersemi didn't want Gardi, but that didn't matter.

She had embarrassed her at the market, and she just plain didn't like her. She was very pretty, and that only made it worse.

While Ama was walking with her basket of fruit, Gersemi stuck out her foot and tripped her, sending the basket, the fruit, and Ama tumbling into a mud puddle. The children laughed, and the men and women did their best to hide it, but they were laughing too.

She was sure that it was because Gersemi was jealous. It wasn't the first time that they had had a confrontation. The incident at the market wouldn't be enough to get Brunhilda to act, but if she thought that Gersemi was after Gardi...

"She had her arm around his neck, and she was stroking his leg." she said. "Of course if you ask her, I'm sure she'll deny it."

The vein on Brunhilda's neck started pulsating rapidly.

"And when did this happen?" she asked.

"She was at the market." she said. "Gardi was there to talk to Egor about making some bows for the voyage. She sat down right next to him."

Brunhilda had never liked Gersemi anyway. The smallest reason would be enough, but now she was after *her man*! She trusted Gardi, but Gersemi was beautiful. She knew that a man in his position could essentially do whatever he pleased, and the temptation of Gersemi might be hard to resist. Marriages had been ruined for less! She wasn't about to let that happen.

"Maybe you shouldn't do anything." said Ama. "After all, it could be innocent."

She knew that Brunhilda had already taken the bait, she was just setting the hook. Gersemi's days were numbered.

She really didn't *like* doing this, but with Brunhilda around, she always had the option.

Ama was a peaceful person. This way she didn't have to get her hands dirty. Deep down, she knew she was lying to herself, but she didn't care. Gersemi should have *known* better. She wouldn't be the first person to disappear, and surely she wouldn't be the last.

"Don't worry about this anymore, Ama." she said. "I'll have a talk with her."

She knew that there would be very little talking, except for the villagers wondering what happened to Gersemi.

"Okay, Brun, if you think that it's best." she said.

"You know that I would never let anyone hurt us, don't you?" she asked.

"Of course, baby." she said. "Jeg elsker dig. Come over here."

Brunhilda came over and gave her a passionate kiss on the mouth.

* * *

She tentatively knocked on the door. After she had calmed down, she felt really bad about what had happened. She could very easily have *killed* him! Just for laughing!

"Come in." said Arve.

She took a deep breath, let it out, and walked through the door.

"Arve..." she said.

"I'm unarmed." he said. "And severely injured."

"I didn't come to fight." she said. "I'm here to apologize."

He started laughing and grabbed his gut.

"Please! Don't make me laugh!" he said. "It's very painful, and I think that's how I got in trouble with you in the first place."

"My temper gets the best of me sometimes, Arve." she said. "I get it from my mother. If daddy didn't stop me, I could have killed you. I'm really sorry, Arve."

"Relax." he said. "Do you really think I would have let you kill me? My arm was coming up as soon as I felt the dagger on my throat."

He knew that this wasn't true, at that moment that it happened, he thought that he was a goner. She probably knew it too.

"All the same, Arve, I am truly sorry." she said. "When you laughed, and everyone else laughed, I saw red."

She moved to a chair near his bed.

"You know that Gardi is talking about leaving me behind." he said. "You fucked me up pretty good."

"I'll talk to him." she said. "I'll take you on my crew and give you enough time to recover."

"Do you think that will work?" he asked.

"Everyone knows that I'm daddy's little girl." she said. "I can talk him into almost anything."

She reached down into a bucket and grabbed a rag that was soaking in the water.

"Take off your shirt."

"Are you flirting with me?" he asked.

"Maybe." she said, smiling.

He took off his shirt gingerly. He really *was* a good looking man. He was solid muscle, and his face was attractive. She *had* said that she would start looking for a man. The gods expected it of her.

She was still in shock about all that had transpired with Idun, and now she had to meet with Danu, another powerful goddess. She had been putting it off, but time was running out before the voyage. She would do it tonight. Even though she was daddy's little girl, she could see an outcome where she would be forbidden to go on the voyage if she didn't meet with Danu. Daddy took the gods very seriously.

She slowly cleaned his wounds, being careful not to hurt him worse than she already had.

"Are you seeing anyone now?" she asked.

She already knew the answer, but she figured that by asking he would know that she was interested.

"Well, there was Magnilda, but we both know how that turned out." he said. "What about you? Are you seeing anyone?"

He couldn't help smirking a little when he asked, but he knew that he *had* to ask. It was all part of the game. He couldn't believe that she was interested after what had happened the previous day.

"No, but I'm looking." she said. "I'm sorry about Magnilda."

Magnilda died in battle during the last raid. She really didn't care either way about Magnilda, but like Arve, she knew that she had to act like she was sorry. This too was part of the game. She realized that Arve probably knew that she was saying it out of obligation, but it still looked like she was doing the right thing.

She finished changing his bandages, and rested her hand on the inside of his leg.

"You know, Lagertha, nobody would ever know that you're looking." he said. "Most of the men are scared of you."

"Well, now you know." she said. "And you're the only one who needs to know. And I know that *you're* not scared of me."

"Perhaps that makes me stupid." he said. "After all, you nearly killed me."

"But I didn't." she said. "And you said that you would never allow me to do it anyway. I can't do anything about that now. I would like it very much if we could put this behind us and move forward."

"I can if you can." he said. "I would rather that we were on friendlier terms."

"Oh, we will be." she said. ""You need to focus on getting better so I can show you just how friendly I can be."

She bent down and gave him a long kiss on the mouth.

"I should go." she said. "If I stick around, I'm liable to tear out your stitches."

He looked at her with amazement. She just laid it all out there. He supposed that she didn't know any other way. There was also no hiding the fact that she was interested.

"I'll look forward to your next visit." he said. "Something tells me that it would have been worth it for you to tear out my stitches."

"No, I've done enough damage already." she said. "It will give you something to look forward to."

"Do me a favor? Talk to Gardi?" he said.

"Consider it done." she said. "I also have an interest in you coming along."

She gave him another kiss and left.

* * *

The sun was heavy on the horizon. He never thought to inquire about what hours she kept, but he had a strong feeling that she would still be around. Whenever he had strong feelings such as this, he acted on them. If she wasn't available, he would spend the night and come back in the morning. He knew some people in Kattegat, and if that didn't work out, he could stay on the boat. He instinctively *knew* that she would be there, and not only that, she would be expecting him.

He entered the tent, and she was lighting incense as before.

"You are late." she said.

"The wind did not cooperate on the way down." he said. "I am sorry."

"Do not worry about it." she said. "After all, who among us controls the wind?"

"Danu? Maybe you?" he said. "Certainly not me."

"If my mother would have wanted you to be here sooner, she would have made it happen." she said. "You are here at the exact moment that you should be. Nothing in this world happens by mistake. Sit."

"That's what Idun told me when my brother was killed." he said. "That nothing happens by mistake."

"It was as true then as it is now." she said. "Do you not believe it to be true?"

"Sometimes I have a hard time believing that everything has been preordained." he said. "There is so much room for error. How could *everything* be fated?"

"How can you deny it?" she asked. "Are you not living proof? How did you get to where you are today?"

"I had a random encounter with Idun in the forest." he said. "I helped her, and she rewarded me with immortality."

"Oh, come now, father, surely you do not believe that it was so simple." she said. "You were destined for this before you were born. I *know* that Idun explained it to you. Surely you do not believe that she gave you such a rich reward simply for collecting her apples and helping her down. You must know by now that your assistance was not required for such a simple task."

"I guess you are right." he said. "I still find it hard to believe. I was an ordinary man. Why would she choose me?"

"Whether you believe it or not, father, you have never been an ordinary man." she said. "And *she* did not choose you. It was fated long ago that *you* would be the one. You do not need to understand the how or the why, you must only do what is expected of you."

Wow, he thought. I'm being scolded by my own daughter. Who is 26 years older than me.

"Has Lagertha been by to see you?" he asked.

"Not yet, but I expect her within the week." she said. "She will meet with Danu tonight."

"What will happen with her?" he asked.

"She will help you." she said. "She will help us all. She has already found a man. His name is Arve."

Gardi started laughing.

"I am sorry, did you say *Arve*?" he asked.

"Yes." she said. "Why is that funny?"

"It is ironic." he said between chuckles. "She nearly killed him a few days ago."

"We do not get to choose who we love." she said. "She is a spirited woman. Perhaps the same passion that made her cut him on the battlefield is what will make her love him."

"She has already gone down that road." he said. "It did not end well for Gunnar."

"Perhaps it will end the same way for Arve." she said quietly. "But it is possible that she will create another descendant of Odin before it is over."

"Is that the reason that she is being helped by the gods?" he asked. "To create more descendants?"

"That is one of the reasons." she said. "There are many. She is *your* daughter. She is the best female warrior since Brenda. I know that you may not want to hear this, but her fate was also decided thousands of years ago."

Again with the fate, he thought.

"What will you tell her when she visits?" he asked. "Will you tell her that you are my daughter?"

"What Lagertha and I discuss will be between the two of us." she said. "What you and I discuss is between us, *alone*. I cannot betray any confidence."

"Should I prepare to explain anything to her?" he asked.

"It is always wise to be prepared for any eventuality." she said. "I must insist that you keep my anonymity. Tell no one that I live."

He was reasonably sure now that she wouldn't tell Lagertha who she was. Did he want her to reveal that information? He wanted Disa to be part of the family, although she didn't seem the family type. Idun told him that it would be her decision if she wanted to reveal her presence. She *had* to know that Gardi would figure it out. She had set him up. For his own good according to her.

"Your secret is safe with me, Disa." he said. "I am only grateful that I am able to see you now."

"I am also grateful, father." she said. "But my participation has *always* been for the greater good, not merely for a family reunion."

"Will she be okay?" he asked.

"She will be fine, as long as she is able to follow instructions." she said. "She is a smart girl. I have no doubt that she will adapt. The gods will be with her."

"That dream…about Brenda, did Danu do that on purpose?" she asked.

"As I said before, nothing in this world happens by mistake." she said. "Everything she saw in that dream was there for a reason. The trial she saw will help her understand the false god. The 'large bird' as she called it was a part of a great disaster that happens more than 1000 years from now. She saw how her mother died, even though she didn't know it was Brenda until you told her. That had a purpose. She will get used to seeing things that happen decades, even centuries from now. She will also see the past. Time will no longer be linear for her. I have seen these things since I was 5 years old. You must help her. It is all new to her, yet you have lived among the gods for more than 50 years. I will help her with her other abilities."

He was amazed. She was the real thing. He hadn't told her anything about Lagertha's dream, yet she knew all of the details.

"I wish I knew more about you, Disa." he said. "It's all a mystery to me. Do you have a husband? Children? Where do you live?"

"I remain a mystery to you for a reason, father." she said. "My life is not for you to know. All that you need to know is that I am here to help. Beyond that, my life will remain private."

She held out her left hand.

"Really?" he asked.

She snapped her fingers and opened her hand again.

He licked her hand. He counted out 6 silver pieces, gave them to her, and left the tent.

Was it because he was asking about her life? Did he push it too far? Maybe after some time she would open up. He knew that it was possible that she would remain distant forever. Was it because of Brenda? She had told him that Brenda had given her the greatest gift that she could hope for. Surely she wasn't holding a grudge because Brenda was his wife. He didn't like the feeling of being powerless.

7

She was waiting in the forest at the same spot where they had met Idun. Nothing was happening. She decided that she would give it another quarter hour, and then leave. There was a steady din of noise, crickets, hoot owls, and other wild beasts.

She looked into the heavens and started picking out constellations. Her father had taught her about the stars. She found Frigga's Distaff, Loki's Torch, The Eagle, and Ratatosk. On the western horizon were Thjazi's Eyes.

She was lost in thought, when the noises of the forest stopped.

She looked up, and Danu stood before her in all her glory. She was a long haired brunette, and she had on a flowing green skirt, split from a matching top by her exposed midriff. She held a sword in her hand, the tip of the blade resting on the ground, and in the crook of her arm rested a golden helmet with wings on the sides. She stood mesmerized for several seconds until Danu spoke.

"Greetings Lagertha, do you know who I am?" she said.

She was speechless. Meeting Idun was one thing, but she could tell just by looking at Danu that she was very powerful. Idun had an aura of peace, but Danu was something different. It wasn't just the sword and the helmet. She knew that Danu could be dangerous. She was at least 6'7" tall, and commanded respect without speaking a word.

She dropped to her knees and bowed her head.

"I am at your service, your holiness." she said.

Unlike Idun, Danu didn't tell her to rise, or make sarcastic jokes about standing on ceremony. She could feel her eyes burning holes in the back of her bowed head.

She was on her knees for a full minute before she felt cold iron on the bottom of her chin. With steady pressure, Danu lifted her chin with the sword and met her eyes.

"So this is what all of the fuss is about?" she said. "I was expecting a woman twice your size wielding Thor's hammer. Are you all that they say you are?"

She didn't know what to say. What had they said she was? Who were *they*? She was very uncomfortable, but she dug deep for her inner strength. She decided that it would be best to show confidence but not too much. She couldn't come off as arrogant, but if Danu was going to kill her, she would go down with a fight.

"Why else would I be here?" she asked.

"You are here of your own choice." she said. "Perhaps *you* should tell *me* why you are here."

"I am here to learn from you." she said. "I was sent by the gods."

"Odin's standards are not as high as mine." she said.

She looked over Lagertha critically. They were right; she was an excellent human specimen. She was beautiful, that would help. She was deferential, to a point. She had a feeling that with humans, she didn't take any shit from anyone.

Danu recognized that she was an imposing figure, and she used it to her advantage. This girl was a little scared, but not terrified like most. That was a good thing. She was pleased with Lagertha, but she wasn't about to let her know it…yet.

"Get on your feet." she said. "We have a lot of work to do."

She slowly rose and brushed off her knees.

"Tell me about your dream." she said.

Of course, Danu already *knew* all about the dream, but she figured that if she had Lagertha tell her about it she could evaluate her psychologically.

Lagertha told her in detail all that she remembered. She hesitated a little bit when relaying the part about Brenda, but she was able to give remarkable details about the rest of the dream. She was smart. That was also a positive. She was starting to like her.

"Now we are going to do an exercise." she said. "What you must do is to clear your mind, and think of nothing except for a certain time. For example, you will clear your mind and think *only* of 45 minutes in the past. You must *feel* it! Thoughts without feelings are useless! Block out everything except for the time that you wish to be. Go ahead, try it."

Lagertha closed her eyes and tried to concentrate on 45 minutes in the past. She was having a hard time focusing and clearing her mind.

"Think of nothing else!" boomed Danu.

Suddenly she found herself walking up a path in the forest heading for the spot that she had hoped to meet Danu. She was stunned, it actually worked!

"Very good!" said Danu, who was walking beside her. "Now try it again with a time of your own choosing."

I guess the sky is the limit, she thought. She cleared her mind and thought about 1000 years in the future. Suddenly she was standing before the largest building she had ever seen. It looked like it was 3 buildings joined together, with rising towers, built with the same small rectangular material as the other buildings, but the tops were a light green color. The roofs of the building were also this shade of green, and angled to a sharp point in the shape of a triangle. There were several chimneys rising through them. The building was 4 stories tall, with 2 more stories on top, getting progressively smaller and ending in a point. There was a large fountain in front of the building with statues of men riding lions and other beasts, and one on top of the fountain of a man with an arm raised in victory. There were several other statues around. Two statues of warriors in armor guarded the entrance. There were people milling around, dressed very strangely, some were riding in incredibly elaborate roofed carts towed by horses.

"It is Frederiksborg Castle." said Danu. "You made quite a leap. 1000 years in the future, but then, I do not need to tell you that. You are the one who brought us here. One of the things you will notice is that people dress differently in the future, as well as the past. If we were to stay for any length of time, we would have to get new clothes, so we do not stand out as we do now."

A man walked past them with strange looking, round, clear objects attached to his face in front of his eyes by wires that went behind his ears. He gave them a strange look.

They are called spectacles, or eyeglasses." said Danu. "They help that man to see more clearly."

"Is he blind?" she asked.

"No, but his eyes are not as sharp as others." she said. "Surely you know people who cannot see as well as you do back home?"

"Yes, I do." she said. "So they have figured out how to improve vision?"

"They have figured out a lot of things, Lagertha." she said.

A woman passed by and gave them a dirty look.

"Why don't you put some clothes on?" she asked.

"We are clothed." said Lagertha.

"You could have fooled me!" she snapped. "My undergarments cover more than what you're wearing!"

Lagertha saw red. Who did this bitch think she was? What business of *hers* was it how they were dressed? *Her* clothes were the ones that looked ridiculous!

She reached to the back of her belt and grabbed her dagger. She saw genuine terror on the woman's face. She started advancing towards her.

Suddenly they were back in the present, in the forest.

"What happened?!" she asked.

"I brought us back here." said Danu. "When you walk through time, *you must not draw attention to yourself*! We are not supposed to be there! If you take anything away from our session today, let it be that."

"I am sorry." she said. "It is my temper. Sometimes I have difficulty controlling it."

"That is something that you must work on, child." she said. "We must blend in when we travel. Save your anger for the battlefield."

"I will try while I am travelling." she said. "I cannot guarantee that I will be so submissive when I am in the present."

"There is no such thing as the present, past, and future." she said. "They are only different levels. I do not expect you to behave meekly during the normal course of your life, but when you walk through time, it is imperative. You cannot change the past, only the future. It is bad practice to change *anything* while you are travelling."

"Idun said that you can help me in battle…not necessarily in the fighting, but in staying alive." she said.

"I think that we both know that you do not need any help with your fighting skills." she said. "Practice walking through time. We will work on keeping you alive in the next session. That is enough for today. Go and see the woman in Kattegat. Come back here in 3 days and I will evaluate your progress."

Lagertha opened her mouth to speak, but Danu was gone.

* * *

She was walking up to the house, hoping to surprise him when she saw them. He had managed to get up, and was standing at the door with her. He must be feeling better, she thought. Gersemi leaned in, wrapped her arms around him, and gave him a kiss on the mouth. He didn't appear to resist. Neither of them saw her. She turned around and walked away.

How could he do this? That little slut had swooped in and put her hooks in him just when they were getting to know each other! She never liked that bitch. Was he really interested in her? She's so *boring*! She doesn't even know how to fight! But she was beautiful, so of course he was interested.

But then, so was Lagertha, and he didn't seem to mind *her* attention the other day. Maybe she *should* have killed him on the battlefield. She would have if daddy didn't stop her.

She thought about what Danu had told her about controlling her anger. That was *only* supposed to be when she was travelling though. Danu couldn't expect her not to react *this* time under the circumstances.

She would take care of Gersemi. Should she let Arve know that she saw them? This was why she didn't like getting involved with men romantically. You could never trust them.

She took a deep breath. Maybe it was innocent. Probably not on *her* side, but could she really fault him for accepting a kiss from a pretty girl? They didn't have a commitment, but she felt that he should know that they would take it to the next level. The only reason that she didn't bed him right there and then was his injuries, and she felt that she had made that pretty clear to him. Did Gersemi make him the same offer? She saw no choice but to eliminate her.

Of course, Gersemi probably had no idea that she was interested, but that didn't matter. All's fair in love and war, she thought.

She decided to go back there and talk to him. She would try to figure out if he was a willing participant, or if he was just playing along. After all, he may not have encouraged it, Gersemi was the kind of girl that would routinely throw herself at men.

She knocked on the door and entered tentatively.

"How are you feeling?" she asked.

"Much better." he said. "I have actually been able to get up and move around a little."

"Good." she said. "Has anyone else been by to visit you?"

"Your father came by yesterday." he said. "I don't know what you told him, but he said I can go on the voyage, thank you."

"Good." she said. "Did anyone else stop by?"

She knows, he thought. She must have seen her. If I deny it, she'll know I'm lying. He really wasn't interested in Gersemi, but she was beautiful, and it was nice to have her visit. He wondered if there was a way that this could play out that didn't involve her dying.

"Gersemi came by a couple of times." he said.

A couple of times?! She's been here more than once?

"Oh, really?" she asked. "What did she want?"

"She said that she was just concerned about my injuries." he said. "She changed the dressings."

So she changed the dressings. That's pretty intimate. She *was* trying to make a move.

"Did you tell her about us?"

"Us?" he asked.

Was he serious? Did he not *know* that she intended to bed him?

"Surely you remember my last visit!" she said. "I all but jumped on top and made love to you!"

"But you tried to kill me the day before." he said. "I haven't forgotten your advances, and believe me, I *am* interested. Gersemi is just concerned about me."

"So concerned that she found it necessary to kiss you on the mouth?!" she said. "That's a hell of a bedside manner!"

"Look, I can't help it if she is a little aggressive." he said. "She's really not my type. You should hear how she talked about *you*!"

"How she talked about *me*?!" she asked. "What did she say?"

He really did it now. He may as well have killed her himself. Why did he bring that up?

"It's nothing really." he said. "She's not like us. She doesn't understand the battlefield. She was upset that you injured me. I tried to explain it to her, but she doesn't understand what it's like. I know that you would never try to kill me."

"Never say never." she said quietly.

So not only is she trying to steal my man, but she's talking shit about me too.

She laid down next to him on the bed. She wrapped one arm around him and put the other between his legs.

"I will give you the benefit of the doubt, Arve." she said. "I am trying to control my anger. It's not easy. I have my mother's temper, and it doesn't always allow me time to think. Are you? Interested in me?"

"You are one of the most beautiful women that I have ever met." he said. "And you have a lot of spirit. You understand me as a warrior. Of course I'm interested in you."

She leaned in and kissed him on the mouth.

"How much better are you feeling?" she asked.

"Much better." he said. "I feel that I can do much more than I was able to do the last time you visited."

Her hand moved to his belt and started loosening it.

8

She was walking alone towards the forest. Brunhilda was about 50 paces behind her, keeping her position concealed. As soon as she got deep enough into the forest, she would close the gap. She had a dagger, an axe, and her sword. She also had some rope, should that become necessary. She was looking forward to this. Ever since Ama had told her about it, she was seething. Suddenly Lagertha appeared.

"Why are you following her?" she whispered.

"She was a little bit too friendly with your father." she said.

"She has a habit of doing that." said Lagertha. "I have a bone to pick with that bitch too."

"Well, you can feel free to pick her bones when *I'm* done with her." she said.

"I'm afraid that I must insist, *mother*." said Lagertha. "*You* can have the leftovers."

Although Brunhilda was technically her stepmother, she had a healthy fear of Lagertha. She stayed out of her way as most people did. This was personal, though.

"And what has she done to you?" she asked.

"The same thing she did to you." she said. "I mean it, Brun. Let it go."

"I wasn't aware that you had a man." she said.

"Well, I do." she said. "So you need to get out of my way."

"Are you going to stop me?" she asked.

"If necessary." she said. "You're my father's wife, and I don't want to hurt you, but don't test me."

She believed her. The problem was that she owed Gersemi an ugly death. She couldn't just let it go. It wasn't in her nature.

"What if we do it together?" she asked.

She didn't want to share this with Brun. She understood why Brun felt that she had to do it, but the justice had to come from her. She had a thought. She grabbed Brun's hand. Suddenly they were at the marketplace the previous morning. Just as quickly Lagertha was gone.

"What the..." she exclaimed.

* * *

As Gersemi approached the clearing about a mile in, she had a feeling of uneasiness. She felt someone's eyes upon her. Suddenly Lagertha appeared before her.

"Go ahead, try to run." she said. "You can't get away."

She turned around and tried to run in the other direction, but Lagertha was there blocking her way.

"How did you do that?!" she cried.

"I told you that you can't escape." she said.

She turned around again, but Lagertha was there. She swung an axe at her head and hit her with the blunt end. She was stunned, but still conscious.

"I would love to take my time with this like mama used to, but you're popular today." she said. "I'm not the only one who wants you dead. I don't know how much time I have."

"But why, Lagertha?" she said. "What have I done?"

"Arve." she said.

"You? And Arve?" she started laughing. "I had no idea!"

As soon as she heard Gersemi laugh, any slim chance she might have had was gone.

"You need to die." she said. "I don't take this kind of thing lightly. Call it a trait passed down from my mother. Besides, I hear that you have committed other sins."

"What?!" she asked.

She searched her mind.

"That thing with Ama at the market?" she said. "It was just a joke!"

She knocked her to the ground.

She kicked her in the face, breaking a tooth off and smashing her nose like a tomato.

"*NO! Please!*" she said. "I'll stay away from him!"

"It's too late for that." she said quietly.

She quickly flipped her over on her stomach, and sat on her head and shoulders. Gersemi was screaming loudly at this point. She put more weight on her head and ground her mouth into the dirt. She made a vertical slice along her spine, then two more slices along her shoulders and her lower back. Then she pulled the skin flaps apart and grabbed her axe. Chopping with the axe, she separated her ribs from her spine and pulled them out through the hole. She carefully set them at a slight angle pointing towards the sky.

Just then Brunhilda appeared at the clearing. Her jaw dropped at the sight of Lagertha. Lagertha wasn't sure what would happen with her little trick, but she had half expected this to happen. After all, time doesn't stop. If she could figure out how to make *that* happen, she'd really be onto something.

"She's still alive." she said. "You can finish it."

Gersemi was screaming her head off. Brunhilda was trying to analyze this unprecedented turn of events.

"How did you do that?!" she asked.

"Call it perseverance." she said. "Does it really matter?"

She kicked Gersemi in the head again.

"Do you want to finish this up, or shall I?" she asked.

Brunhilda approached Gersemi. She grabbed one of the ribs and twisted.

Gersemi wailed and started kicking wildly, but she was a few inches short of connecting with Brunhilda. She kept hitting her own exposed ribs which made her scream even louder. Brunhilda took her sword and buried it into the back of her left knee and twisted. She howled as her lower leg was separated from her body. She lifted Gersemi's head and stared into eyes.

"I've always wondered what someone would look like without a face." she said. "How about you, Lagertha? Would you want to see that?"

"I've already seen it." she said absently.

Already seen it? Had she *really* already done this?

"Please don't do this Brunhilda!" she wailed. "Have mercy!"

"What difference does it make?" she asked. "You're dead already, you just don't know it. I *am* grateful that you can still feel pain, though."

She took her dagger and made slices on both sides of her face, then one across the top of her forehead. Gersemi was screaming her head off. She grabbed her hair, and wedged her fingers inside the wound on her forehead and pulled. Her face came clean off, leaving the front of her skull exposed, her eyes darting back and forth rapidly, and her tongue flapping wildly as she shrieked.

"You're too loud." said Brunhilda.

She reached in and grabbed her tongue and yanked hard. It came out about 4 inches, and she sliced it off. Gersemi involuntarily urinated and passed out.

She was still alive, but Lagertha had taken most of the fun out of it. It was pointless now, she was beyond pain. She reached in and yanked out her lungs, and plunked them on top of the ribs. She was pissed at Lagertha. At least Gersemi got her ugly death. She took her head off with the sword for good measure.

"We need to get rid of the body." said Lagertha.

"I'm still trying to figure out how you got up here!" she said. "You were standing right next to me, then we seemed to go back in time, then you were gone! I relived my day, right up until the point when we ran into each other, but you weren't there! Next thing I know, you're here, finishing up with her! How did you do that?!"

"I have talents that nobody knows about." she said. "Do you *really* want to sit here and discuss it? Now? Or do you want to cover our tracks?"

"This conversation is *not* over!" she said.

"Yes it is." she said.

She looked at Lagertha. She didn't have any delusions that she could make the girl do anything that she didn't want to do. She would never admit it to anyone out loud, but she knew that she was no match for Lagertha.

But how did she do that? They went back in time! And somehow, Lagertha went forward! She couldn't believe it when she got to the clearing and saw Lagertha in the process of carving her up. *How did she do that?* Maybe Gardi knew.

She grabbed the head and the leg, and Lagertha threw the torso over her shoulder. Brunhilda started heading for the river, but Lagertha stopped her.

"No." she said. "There's no use letting all this meat go to waste."

Letting all this meat go to waste? What was she talking about? Was she planning on eating her?

They walked about another half mile in and Lagertha stopped. They heard some low growling.

"We're here." she said.

A wolf came up to Lagertha and started licking her hand. There were a lot of human remains in the area, cleaned to the bone. Several other wolves appeared. The biggest one started growling at Brunhilda and opened its mouth showing sharp yellow teeth. Brunhilda started slowly backing away.

"Broderic!" said Lagertha. "Stop! I have brought you dinner."

She walked over and started scratching the big wolf between the ears. He sat down on his haunches and looked down meekly at her feet.

Brunhilda was speechless. First she somehow takes me back in time, moves *forward* in time to beat her to Gersemi, now she's as one with the wolves. What other secrets does she have? This was very disturbing, and what was worse, she didn't have the nerve to ask for an explanation.

"I take all of my victims out here for them." she said quietly.

"C-Can we go back now?" she managed to get out.

"Of course." she said. "Eat up, boys and girls! And Brun? Did you *really* want to ask me about what happened earlier?"

Broderic snapped at her again.

She would grateful just to come out of this encounter alive. Something was going on with her step daughter, and she didn't want any part of it.

"N-No, I'm good." she said. "Whatever it is, it's between you and the gods."

"You are exactly right, *mother*." she said. "Oh, and Brun? Absolutely *nobody* hears about this. Do I make myself clear?"

She couldn't speak, so she just slowly nodded her head.

"That's good." she said. "Because I would hate to have to hurt you. And we both *know* that I could. These wolves are always hungry. I think Broderic likes you. If there ever is a next time, you would be wise to just back off like I asked you to do in the first place. There is no need for competition between mother and daughter, don't you agree?"

"Y-Yes, Lagertha." she said. "It won't happen again. I am truly sorry that I got in your way. The end result was the same. I am grateful to you for helping me with this."

"I understand why you wanted to do it yourself." she admitted. "Next time you will listen to me. If I say that she is *mine*, it means that she is mine."

"Y-Yes, Lagertha." she said.

They walked back to the village in silence.

* * *

When the fisherman that she asked for directions started flirting with her, she gave him a blank stare. It was the kind of a stare that told him that she could cut him in half without thinking twice. She towered over him by at least a half a foot, and she was solid muscle.

"You're from the north, aren't you?" he asked.

She just stared back at him, boring 2 holes into his skull.

"I-It's the 3rd tent past the blacksmith on the right." he said nervously.

She turned around and started walking towards town. She walked into the tent and the woman was sitting peacefully in the corner facing the wall.

"I was…" she started.

The woman held up one finger in protest, stopping Lagertha instantly. A full minute went by before woman turned around.

"Greetings, Lagertha." she said. "I have been expecting you."

The woman is obviously blind, how does she know who it is? She's been expecting me?

"How do you know my name?" she asked.

"I'm a seer, I see things." she replied. "And how are *they*?"

Lagertha instinctively knew that she was talking about the wolves. But how would she know that?

They are fine." she said. "How do you know about them?"

"I can smell them on you." she said. "They raised me."

"Really?" she asked. "How did that happen?"

"I was abandoned in the forest at an early age." she said. "Danu sent Flidais the goddess of the forest to help me, and I fell under their protection. The same woman who abandoned me also blinded me. That's when I started seeing things for the first time."

"And who was this woman?" she asked.

"You are asking the wrong questions, child." she said. "I see that you have already tried it on your own. That stunt with Gersemi. I thought that Danu told you to try to control your anger."

"She said that it only applies when I am travelling." she said. "She understands that it is too much to ask when I am in my own life."

"While that may be true, it is silly to kill someone over an imagined offense, is it not? And you *were* travelling, you just did not go very far." she said. "I understand that you cannot change who you are. I knew your mother. Some things never change. I only ask that you try to think before you act."

"But I *did* think." she said. "I thought about it for an entire day."

"But her fate was sealed the minute you saw her with Arve." she said. "You may say that you thought about it, but all that you *really* thought about was how you were going to kill her."

"You said that you knew my mother." she said. "What was she like?"

"Still the wrong question." she said. "I am not the person to tell you about your mother. The last time I saw her was before my 5th year. Let's talk about travelling."

Mama must have been young when this woman met her. She had to be at least 50 years old. Why would a woman from Kattegat know her mother? She said that the wolves raised her. *Her* wolves. Was she from Skagen? Something in her demeanor made Lagertha know not to push the issue.

"I think that I have figured out how Danu can teach me to stay alive." she said. "I'm sure you know that I did it while I was with Gersemi."

"Yes, you are a smart girl, Lagertha." she said. "It worked that time, but I must say that it was rather sloppy. You will need to practice. An actual opponent could easily have killed you. Gersemi was certainly no test. Danu will work with you on that."

Lagertha thought that she had done pretty well. She had fun bouncing around in time. She had found a trick to clear her mind. She focused on the vastness of space and time and arrived at the point where she wanted to be.

"My focus is getting better and quicker." she offered.

"You must *feel* it, child." she said. "There will be more distractions on the battlefield. You *know* that. Thoughts are good, but without feelings they are useless. *You must feel it!*"

"Danu said the same thing." she said. "What exactly does that mean?"

"You must feel the feelings of being in the moment." she said. "You must be there in every way before you get there. When you master that, you will have mastered travelling. Then all doors will be open to you."

"I will continue to practice." she said. "We will be leaving for the raids soon. Is there any way to *stop* time?"

She thought about what happened with Brun, and it would have been much easier to just put her in suspended animation while she dealt with Gersemi.

"Please tell the children that I miss them." she said. "My name is Disa."

She held out her left hand.

So that's it? She's dismissing me? She's not even going to answer my question?

She snapped her fingers and opened her hand again.

"6 silver pieces." she said.

Lagertha licked her hand and counted out the money.

9

"Can you make it?" he asked expectantly.

"I think so." he said. "As long as it's okay with Alfdis."

"Must you ask her permission?" he asked. "Are you not your own man?"

He knew that he could go if he wanted to. He was trying in vain to keep the peace at home. Erika wanted to move back to Denmark, and he couldn't blame her. Alfdis was beside herself. She saw it as a rejection of Christ. Magna was also talking about leaving.

He could tell that they both missed Denmark, and neither were too interested in Christianity. Privately, they were both still devoted to the Norse gods. Freki wasn't devoted to anything except science and learning.

He wanted to go to the party. Some of the brightest minds in Wessex would be there. He would find a way to smooth things over with Alfdis and get out of the house for the night.

"Of course I am my own man." he said. "You don't understand Henry. You've never been married. It requires some ingenuity to handle a woman who is upset. Two of her daughters want to go back to Denmark."

"What does one thing have to do with the other?" he asked.

"Have you ever been with a woman, Henry?" he asked. "Had a girlfriend?"

"Yes, but the ones that I have picked didn't believe in fairy tales." he replied. "You don't want to miss this party, Freki."

"I will be there." he said. "I'll find a way."

"Why do you need to 'find a way'?" he asked. "Why can't you just tell her you're going? Hell, invite her along. She might learn something."

Freki started laughing.

"You don't know what a disaster that would be!" he said. "She would be stationed at the bar preaching to anyone who would listen to her! No, I'll come alone. I'll be nervous enough as it is."

"There's nothing to be nervous about, Freki." he said. "These are *our* people. You can relax and be yourself. Are things any better? Between the two of you?"

"I feel like we're just hanging on for the sake of the children." he said. "Honestly, I feel like we're growing apart. What's worse is that I'm starting to lose interest in fixing it."

"Well, I wish you luck, my friend." he said. "I find myself too busy to accommodate a permanent woman."

"It wasn't always like this." he said.

He thought back to the time when he and Alfdis met back in Denmark. She was so proud to be with the son of Gardi. They were in love. She was very religious even then. She worshipped the Norse gods, perhaps more than she worshipped Christ now.

It didn't bother him the same way then that it did now. Of course, back then he was an uneducated pagan. Not that he was any kind of genius, but he understood how things worked now. There was no benevolent 'god' watching over them. It could all be explained by science. Well, maybe not *all*, but that was only because there was still so much to learn.

He looked forward to going to the party. Alfdis would have to understand. Or she wouldn't. He really didn't care. He deserved this. He had been listening to her prattle on about Jesus for years now. He couldn't be less interested.

What had happened to her? She had turned into the kind of woman that *needed* something greater than herself to believe in. It didn't have to make sense. She swallowed what the church told her whole, and without question. What kind of person doesn't require some kind of logical explanation? She called it faith. He called it delusion.

He knew that he could never believe as she did. He didn't even believe in the *Norse* gods that he had grown up with anymore. Of course it was the same with them. The Danish people believed in their gods without question as well. Why did people need gods? So they would have someone to blame, he thought.

"Stop by my place at 6." he said. "We'll go over there together."

"I'll see you then." he said.

* * *

"I'm just going fishing." he said.

He hated lying to her, but he certainly couldn't tell her where he was really going. She knew that he liked to fish, so he figured that if he told her that, she wouldn't make a fuss. He couldn't be more wrong.

"Don't you understand that we're facing a crisis here?" she said. "Their *souls* are at risk!"

"Erika is 31 years old. Magna is 29. They're old enough to do what they want." he said exasperated. "You can't control their lives forever."

"Don't you understand how *important* this is?" she said. "If they go back to the Norse gods, they will never enter the Heavenly Kingdom!"

"Is that what your god does?" he asked. "Punishes people?"

"He is a forgiving God!" she said. "He died on the cross to wash away our sins. But we are to hold no other gods before him! And he's not *my* God, he's *our* God!"

"You may claim him, but I do not." he said. "Some of the stories are entertaining, but it's *fiction*! Made up by men that lived hundreds of years ago."

"Do not say that!" she said. "You *must* claim him as your savior! It's the only way! I'm serious about what I said earlier. We need to validate our marriage."

I thought that's what the kids were for." he said. "You have been my wife in every way for the last 32 years. I don't need to reaffirm it to a god that I don't believe in."

"But *I* don't consider it valid!" she cried. "We were never married in the eyes of God! What's worse, they performed the ceremony before *false* gods! I mean it, Freki. I'll have it annulled."

"I'm leaving." he said. "Don't wait up."

With that, he walked out the door, careful not to slam it on the way out.

He got to Henry's house, and they had a drink before they left.

"Are you ready for this?" asked Henry.

"Sure." said Freki. "You said that there's nothing to be nervous about."

"The thing is, Freki, some of them know that you used to be a Viking." he said. "They're pretty open minded people, but it doesn't mean that they're not prejudiced."

"*Now* you tell me this!" he said. "What does the fact that *I* used to be a *Viking* have to do with anything?"

"It's not so much that." he said. "It's that you're from Denmark. They consider it to be a backwards country. Just be yourself. You're a smart man. After they get to know you, you'll be fine."

"So now I must prove myself?" he asked.

"In the natural order of things, they will realize that you're intelligent." he said. "That you're not one of *them*. You know...the people you grew up with."

"So I must deny my heritage?" he asked.

"Just relax, and be yourself." he said. "There's nothing to worry about. *I* know that you're not like *those people*, the rest of them will figure it out quickly enough."

He didn't know what to think. He had distanced himself from his old life, but he loved his family and the people he left behind in Denmark. Did he need to put on an act for these people? Henry was probably right; they would realize that he was intelligent.

They got to the house and there were several people standing around drinking and talking. There was a woman in an animated discussion with a man with a pointed beard.

"Impossible." he said. "The earth is at least twice its size. It could not possibly orbit around the sun. It's basic physics! You can't be serious, Annabel!"

"And how do you know how big the sun is, Edward?" she said. "Have you been there?"

"Don't be ridiculous." he said. "It's common knowledge! You can tell just by looking!"

"That depends on how far away it actually is." said Freki. "Do you think that all of the stars are the size of ants?"

"And who are you?" he asked in disgust.

"I'm Freki." he replied. "I'm a friend of Henry's."

"That explains a lot." he retorted. "You're the *Viking*?"

Annabel gave him a curious look. So this is what a Viking looks like, she thought.

"Not anymore." he said. "Please don't tell me that you actually think the sun is 3 inches wide."

"Of course not, you dolt." he said. "But I know that the earth is bigger."

"And how do you know that?" he asked.

"Like I said, it's common knowledge." he said. "People have been floating Annabel's heliocentric theories for years. It's pure delusion."

"So you know how big the earth is?" he asked. "You've studied Eratosthenes?"

"Of course." he said.

"And did Eratosthenes also measure the sun?" he asked.

"And how would he do that?" asked Edward.

"He couldn't." replied Freki. "Which brings me to my original question. How far away is the sun?"

"How should *I* know?" he roared.

"Indeed, how can any of us know?" said Freki. "Eratosthenes also calculated the distance to the sun, but there's been a dispute over the wording, which could make it one of two very different answers. The distance could either be 4,080,000 stadia or 804,000,000 stadia depending on how you interpret it. Quite a difference. Either way, the sun is at least a million miles away. This certainly supports the argument that it could be larger than the earth. I happen to believe that Annabel is right. The sun supports life on earth. Without it, we would all freeze to death. The crops wouldn't grow. The sun supports the earth, and the earth has no significant effect on the sun. Why would the sun orbit the earth? It makes no sense."

Annabel was enthralled. She had never seen anyone take Edward on and win. The way Freki explained it to him, even an idiot would understand. He had a way of breaking it down to the simplest terms.

"My friend, how can a smaller object pull a larger one into its orbit?" he asked, exasperated.

"And how do you know that the sun is smaller? You're so set against the heliocentric theory that you look at nothing else." he said. "Do you know why?"

"Because it's the truth!" he boomed." The earth is the center of the universe!"

He was beginning to turn red, and he was twirling the end of his beard wildly.

"The geocentric theory is proclaimed as the truth in the *bible.*" he said. "*That's* why people don't question it. I've learned about many religions. I haven't found one yet that relies on research or truth. They count on people believing without question. Are you one of those people?"

Annabel had to turn the other way to try to stifle her laughter. This guy was great!

Edward looked as if he was about to explode.

"Did worship a sun god as a child?" he asked.

"I worshiped many gods." he said quietly. "Now don't pray at all."

"And how often have you participated in human sacrifice?" he asked. If he could prove that Freki was a barbarian, he could discredit him.

"Not that it has anything to do with the subject we were discussing, but I can see why you don't want to continue with that. The Norse people gather at Uppsala every nine years to worship their gods." he said. "They make sacrifices of humans as well as many other animals. It used to be a devout ceremony, but now it's a festival of debauchery. I haven't been there in 22 years. I've been there in the past for the gathering, but I have never participated in human sacrifice."

"And how many men have you killed, *Viking*?" he asked.

"Several, but not as many as my brother." he replied calmly.

He looked directly into Edward's eyes as if to say that he would have no problem killing again.

Edward went from bright red to pale white in a matter of seconds.

Just then another man walked up.

"You must come and meet Philipp, Ed." he said. "He's the one I told you about. He studies plants."

"Good." he huffed. "I've been looking for intelligent conversation all night."

He walked off grateful to get away from the Viking. What kind of lunacy was that? The earth orbiting the sun! He was disappointed in Annabel. Thomas had come just in time. He couldn't think of an argument to put the Viking in his place, and what was worse he was scared of him. How did that man get into this party in the first place?

"I really didn't need rescuing, but I appreciate it all the same." she said.

"Your rescue was not my primary objective." he said. "I *do* believe that the earth orbits the sun. Saving a damsel in distress was just a bonus."

She giggled meekly. This man was fascinating! And he used to be a Viking? She had always viewed them as such horribly dense creatures.

"So what was it like?" she asked. "To be a Viking?"

"Until I moved here, I didn't know anything else." he said. "It was quite an adventure. My father…"

He stopped. I really shouldn't get into that, he thought. Annabel was attractive, and she seemed to be interested in him. Besides he couldn't really get into religion after dressing Edward down like that. He really didn't want to get into religion at all, but it was inevitable if he talked about his father.

"Well, my half-brothers and sister were the real warriors." he said.

"Your sister?" she asked.

"We had what were called 'shield maidens'." he said. "Basically a female Viking. Many women from Denmark like this type of life. My half-sister Lagertha is by far the most dangerous person in the family."

"And how does that happen?" she asked.

"It's the culture." he said. "She also inherited certain traits from her mother and my father that made her a warrior. She probably was doomed to that life from the start."

"So you believe in genetics?" she asked.

"To a point." he said. "I also believe that much of it comes from upbringing."

"Then how do you explain yourself?" she asked. "You're not like that."

"Not now." he said. "But there was a time. I also had a different mother. By all accounts, she was a gentle woman."

"You didn't know her?" she asked, puzzled.

"She died in childbirth when I was born." he said quietly. "My father's other wife, Brenda raised me, but she didn't play a big part. That's where genetics comes in. Brenda was a shield maiden, and a fierce one. All of her children turned out like her, but I am different."

"His other wife?" she asked.

"My father is a powerful man." he said. "Nobody begrudged him a second wife. My mother was the first. He has 2 wives now."

"But he must be in his 80s by now!" she said. "How does he do it? *Why* does he do it?"

"My father is...well different." he said. "It's hard to explain. In many ways he's younger than me."

This was always difficult. Explaining his father. At least he wasn't here for her to see. He had two children that were technically older than Gardi.

"Well, let's hope that you're right about the genetics!" she said. "Not that you look old, you're very appealing."

"So are you Annabel." he said.

She didn't seem the type to fish for compliments, but it was always best to play it safe in these situations.

She was probably somewhere around 20 years younger than him, but it didn't seem to bother her in the least.

"Thank you, Freki!" she said. "Most of the men at this party wouldn't know enough to compliment a woman's appearance. It's very refreshing! Do you need to be anywhere later on?" she asked.

He thought about Alfdis. The *last* thing he wanted to do was to go back and deal with her. He was having a good time, and enjoying Annabel's company. He suspected that she asked about his plans because she wanted to include herself in them.

"Not really." he said.

"So what's your situation?" she asked. "Are you available? Is there a Mrs. Freki?"

"Yes, I'm married." he said.

"Happily?" she asked.

"No. I actually don't expect it to last much longer." he said. "She's converted to Christianity."

"And what about you?" she asked. "Are you religious?"

"I don't believe in *anything* anymore." he said.

"Well, I feel that the man/woman thing was never intended to last forever." she said. "That's what the *church* believes. I believe that we only get together to procreate…and have a little fun. After a while, we end up not liking each other very much. It's inevitable. *Nobody* is supposed to be with one person forever."

"And what about you? Are you married?" he asked. "Are you religious?"

"No, I'm not married, but I was raised to be religious." she said. "When I got older and saw how the world really works, and I stopped believing. What was it like to be a pagan?"

"It was interesting." he said. "I have found that most religions have the same message, and the same expectations. Blind faith above all. Most naturally occurring events in Denmark are attributed to the gods. I think that it gives people a reason to believe. When they can say that Thor causes the thunder and lightning, or that Odin cast Thjazi's eyes into the heavens to create a new constellation, it becomes easier. That's why they make up the stories, it's the same as the Christians. Of course, all of that can be explained scientifically, but they don't know science in Denmark."

"Well, we have people here that believe that constellations were created by gods too." she said. "The vast majority still believe in the bible. It's the great lie that has enslaved so many. I prefer to be free."

"I prefer to *know*." he said. "To me, belief in gods is pure speculation. It's wishful thinking. I believe in science. Knowing the truth for a fact is the only way to be truly free."

"Then you are truly free." she said. "To do *whatever* you want."

She grabbed his hand and slung an arm around him.

"Would you like to go back to my place?" she asked.

He couldn't think of a reason not to. He and Alfdis seemed to be over.

She had told him a few days ago that she didn't consider their marriage valid, since they didn't marry before her new god. She insisted that they go through another ceremony at her church. He had told her that he wouldn't. She said that if he wouldn't that she would get their marriage annulled. He told her to do what she had to do, and she broke down crying.

His marriage was over. She wanted to renew their vows in a place that he didn't believe in. He no longer wanted to vow anything to her. She had threatened to have it annulled. He didn't care either way.

"I would love to." he said. "Let's get out of here."

10

"It was just weird!" she said. "There's something going on with that girl. *How did she do that?*"

Ama looked at her with concern. She usually didn't tell her about her escapades, but she couldn't keep this to herself. Ama didn't want to hear about it. All that gore. It always made her feel guiltier for setting things in motion.

Of course Brun had no idea that she had been set up. It was one of the things that she truly loved about her. Something told her that even if she knew, she would do it anyway. She was so in love that she would do *anything* for Ama. Sometimes she thought that she loved her even more than she loved *Gardi*. He was very happy with the arrangement, and why wouldn't he be? It was every man's dream.

"So…you went back in time?" she asked. "Are you sure?"

Now that *Ama* was asking, she didn't know. Could it all have been a dream? Was Lagertha working some kind of dark magic? She would have gone and checked the body for confirmation, but they left it with the wolves. And the wolves! What was up with that?

"I think so…" she said. "Now you have me questioning myself! Could it all have been a dream? An illusion?"

"Anything is possible." she said. "Have you seen Gersemi around?"

"No. And people have been asking about her." she said. "No, I *know* that this happened, Ama. Do you think that maybe Gardi...no, why would he? Is she working with the gods?"

"If this happened, and you seem to think it did, the gods are *definitely* involved." she said. "We'll ask Gardi. It wouldn't surprise me. She *is* daddy's little girl."

"I've never heard of a god that can travel through time." said Brunhilda. "Has she been learning magic? That's the only explanation."

"Well, she *did* go to that seer in Kattegat a few days ago." she said. "The same one that Gardi has been seeing."

"And why is he seeing her?" she asked. "He's always told me that seers give him the creeps."

"Idun told him to go." said Ama. "You don't think she's involved? With Lagertha?"

"Like you said, anything is possible." she said. "If someone was going to be blessed by the gods, why not one of us?"

Now Ama *was* concerned. Why wouldn't he help his wives first? Why would he pick that uncivilized cunt? Not that Brun was much better, but Lagertha was a barbarian. Brun had her soft side, even if she never revealed it to anyone but her. And Gardi *knew* that. Forget about Lagertha or Brun, why not *her*?

Just then Gardi walked in the door.

"I think we need to have a talk." said Ama.

Brunhilda stood in the corner with her arms crossed.

"What about, sweetie?" he asked.

"Your daughter." she said.

"Which one?" he asked.

Brun started to speak, but Ama held up her hand. They both knew that it would be better if she did the talking.

"Like you don't know!" she said. "The one who has been blessed by the gods!"

He looked quickly away, then went directly to her eyes.

"All of my children have been blessed by the gods." he said.

"Let's not play games." she said. "We *all* know that something is going on with Lagertha."

"What happened?" he asked.

"Without going into too much detail, she's been travelling through time." she said. "Brun witnessed it firsthand."

"If you're going to make such an accusation, you really *should* go into detail." he said. "I can't go on a hunch. Besides, if she travelled through time, what business is that of yours? And what does it have to do with me?"

"You're the only person I know that has a personal connection with the gods." she said. "Why did you pick her? Why not one of us?"

"You give me too much power." he said. "What makes you think that *I* pick anything? And which one of the gods is a time traveler?"

He hadn't said anything that could implicate either of them. He had a much easier time handling these two than he ever did with Astrid and Brenda. What did Lagertha do?

"Did Idun help her?" she asked.

"You know very well that I cannot discuss what goes on between us." he said "I told you that 25 years ago when I married you. Are you even sure that this happened?"

Suddenly she wasn't. Could Brun have imagined it all? She had a wild imagination, and she tended towards exaggeration. It seemed that there was far too much detail for her to fabricate this event. She knew that the conversation with Gardi was all but over. He wasn't going to talk about it anymore. If he could get her to question herself, he got the upper hand, and he never forfeited it.

Brunhilda spoke up for the first time.

"Was Brenda part of the wolf clan?" she asked.

"As a matter of fact she was." he said. "What does that have to do with anything?"

"Your daughter is incredibly chummy with the wolves." she said. "We went out to the forest to dispose of a body, and she led us to the pack. She was petting them and they were licking her hand. They growled and snapped at me, but they loved her. It was like they were her family."

He immediately thought of Disa. He did his best to keep his composure. He knew about the time travel, but this was news to him. How long had this been going on? Was it Disa? He would have to talk to Lagertha about this, and being more careful about who she let see her walk through time.

"Well, she's full of surprises." he said. "I don't know what happened, or whose body you were disposing of, and I don't *want* to know. You will keep all of this talk between us. Do I make myself clear?"

They both looked demurely towards their feet.

"Yes, Gardi." they replied in unison.

"You would do well to remember that Lagertha is a dangerous woman." he said. "Being married to me only affords you so much protection. Don't poke the tiger."

So we are back where we started, thought Ama. He *knows* something. She still hadn't mastered how to make him talk. Sex didn't work, threats didn't work, and talking didn't work. She didn't have that kind of power over him. Nobody did. He wouldn't do anything that he didn't want to do.

Even if she and Brun teamed up on him they wouldn't get any answers, the gods knew that they had tried that approach. She and Brun would have to regroup and try to come up with another plan.

Occasionally after sex he let his guard down a little, but if that happened, he would only give enough to make them want more. He would never tell anything that he didn't want to. She admired that about him, but it was also frustrating.

He was the only man that either of them had ever been with, and he had that power as well. Maybe he will tell us on his own, she thought. That was wishful thinking.

The only way he would ever talk is if he had to. She had heard the stories about when he admitted to his immortality. He had no choice that time. He had been 'killed' in battle, only to rise again. He had to come clean with his crew. He had kept the secret for months.

If Lagertha made a mistake, and something had to be said, would he talk? Or would he leave that up to her? He was a big believer in personal responsibility, and he would probably make her tell it herself. But would she? If she didn't, they may never know.

For now, Ama had a keen interest in Lagertha and whether she had mystical powers or not.

"I need to go to Kattegat." he said.

"When will you be back?" asked Brunhilda.

"Within a few days." he said.

"Are you going to see *her*?" she asked. "The seer?"

"What business is that of yours?" he asked.

"I just find it strange." she said. "You always told us that you don't like seers. That you don't trust them."

"This one is different." he said. "She's helping me with some things that I can't figure out on my own."

They both started laughing.

"Things that you can't figure out on your own?!" asked Ama. "If you don't want to tell us, that's ok, elsker, but don't treat us like we're stupid. It's insulting. I don't believe that there is *anything* that *you* can't figure out."

"And why do you think that is?" he asked. "It's because I always have people around me to help. How do you think I got to where I am today?"

"I think that you had a lot of help from Idun." she said. "Without her, you would have been dead years ago."

"*Now* who's being insulting?" he asked.

"I didn't mean any offense, and I'm grateful every day that you have been blessed." she said. "Still, you have to admit that without her, you wouldn't be where you are now."

"Sometimes I wish that I had never met her." he said quietly.

She knew that he was telling the truth. It wasn't that he was unhappy, he just didn't like all of the attention. He had told her that sometimes it felt like the immortality was as much of a curse as a blessing. Whatever happened, he would have to go on. He had already lost so many of his friends and family, yet he stayed 28 years old and didn't die. She and Brunhilda were both older than him now.

She walked over to him, closely followed by Brunhilda. They took their usual positions, Brun on the right, and Ama on his left. They wrapped their arms around him and sat quietly.

"You know that both of us love you, and we wouldn't have it any other way." she said. "We just want you to be happy."

"I don't want to hear any more talk of Lagertha…about this thing that she may or may not be able to do. The gods are everywhere. Do you think that I'm the only one that they have ever helped? Her blood goes back to the wolves, as yours goes to the bears. Just like yours goes back to the owls." he said, nodding at Brun and Ama respectively.

"But I'm not friendly with the bears, and you don't see an owl sitting on Ama's shoulder." she said.

Ama looked at Brun sternly and shook her head back and forth, silently signaling her to stop speaking.

"That is not my point." he said. "Both of you have fine qualities that complement the other spectacularly. If Lagertha has powers that are beyond natural, you should be proud and grateful.

You should not question them. We all need a little magic in our lives."

"I *am* grateful." said Ama. "Whatever is happening with her is a blessing."

She knew that the time for questions was over with Gardi, even if Brun didn't. She *would* figure it out later.

They would both be gone soon on the voyage, and she knew some people who might be able to help her.

She leaned over and started kissing Brun as her hand drifted between Gardi's legs.

* * *

"You don't think that it was good?" asked Lagertha. "I was one step ahead of her the whole time!"

Danu looked her over. She was being very familiar. It was bordering on disrespect. Yes, she was able to fool that little twit, but she would have been able to defeat her even without her powers. That was almost certainly true with almost any human that she fought. Even if she didn't admit it to Lagertha, given what little experience she had, she had done enough to survive.

Her eyes started burning bright red.

"You will show me the respect that I deserve, young lady." she said. "ON YOUR KNEES!"

She fell to her knees and bowed her head.

What was that with her eyes? Danu wasn't anywhere near as fun as Idun. What had she done? She was only talking normally to her. Maybe that was the problem.

"I am *not* one of your Viking buddies!" she roared. "I am a goddess, and you will treat me with respect."

A full three minutes passed before she felt the cold iron under her chin. The pressure that Danu applied brought Lagertha's eyes to meet her own. Because she was so tall, she seemed even more imposing. Her eyes were still burning red.

"You will not speak to me as though I am an ordinary person." she said. "I am not. I could end your life without a second thought, and feel nothing. Do you understand me?"

Lagertha started nodding her head slowly. Danu's eyes slowly returned to normal.

"What you did with Gersemi was unacceptable." she said. "You must become better. You may rise to your feet."

She slowly got up and dusted her knees off. She would have to be more careful with Danu. She felt something with her that she had never known. Fear.

"Brunhilda is a loose end now." she said. "Loose ends are a problem. Do you want to kill your stepmother? Because *that* is what we do with loose ends. She has already told Gardi and Ama. *Nobody* must know about this. Fortunately for you, Gardi has already spoken to her. I have been assured that it will go no further. We must get you ready for the voyage. Are you ready to go to work?"

"Do I have a choice?" she asked.

She felt the flat end of the blade smack her in the cheek before she got the words out. She fell to the ground, and Danu's foot was instantly on her chest, holding Lagertha down as the blade found the bottom of her chin. It punctured her skin neatly as she let out a gasp.

"Shall we end this now?" she asked. "It makes little difference to me. They said that you are smart. I have found little evidence of that. What I see is a petulant little girl used to getting her own way."

The blade inched deeper into her throat. Blood trickled down, and ran like a tiny river between her breasts. Lagertha raised her hands in surrender. It was not a feeling that she had ever known. Danu didn't let up. Her eyes were burning red again. A wicked grin slowly grew on her face.

This is it, she thought. I'm going to die right here simply for questioning with her.

Not without a fight!

She grabbed the blade with both hands and pulled with all her might. It didn't budge. Blood ran down her arms as the sword cut deeply into her fingers. She tried twisting, but it only carved her hands up more. She tried kicking, but Danu was so tall that she didn't even come close. Finally she let go of the blade.

"Go ahead!" she panted. "Kill me!"

"They also said that you are a fighter." she said. "It is disappointing how easily you give up. I find it hard to believe that you have lived this long, as weak as you are."

"I'm only human." she gasped.

Danu was laughing uproariously on the inside, but her face betrayed nothing. The girl was funny! Her sense of humor may very well have saved her life. Yes, she was only human! Sometimes Danu forgot that about her subjects. She expected only the very best from the humans that she worked with, and if they fell short, it was usually the end for them. It was a great privilege to have her attention, and she didn't suffer foolishness. There were the Norse gods to consider as well. It wasn't always a friendly relationship. There was a delicate peace in the balance, and she didn't wish to break it for this girl. Danu was Odin's mother. He had grown so powerful that sometimes he forgot that.

"Get up!" she demanded.

Lagertha rose to her feet quickly, relieved that she was still alive.

"Give me your hands." she said.

Lagertha held them out. Danu took them and examined them closely.

"I am sure that I do not have to tell you how stupid it was to grab the blade, do I?" she asked.

"No, your highness." she said quietly.

Danu smiled broadly. *That's* more like it.

Lagertha didn't dare try to explain her reasoning that she was fighting for her life. It would certainly be seen as making an excuse, and therefore disrespectful.

Danu looked to the heavens.

"Airmed, hear my plea." she said. "Take pity on this foolish girl and make her hands whole again. She knows not what she does…she may yet learn."

Suddenly a woman appeared. She had long red hair, green eyes, and a flowing green gown to match. In her hand was a small bowl, and she was softly mashing the contents with a golden spoon. She looked at Lagertha puzzled.

"What has she done?" she asked.

"The fool thought that she could wrestle my sword away by grabbing the blade." she said. "We were having…a disciplinary problem."

"Why would you do such a thing, child?" she asked.

She had a look of genuine concern on her face. Lagertha could tell that she was not like Danu. She was more like Idun. How had this happened? In the space of a week she had met 3 goddesses. What should she tell her? She was still wary of Danu.

"She is right, my lady, I am a fool." she said. "I do not know what I was thinking."

"Come to me and give me your hands, elsker." she said.

She spread the mixture from the bowl all over her hands. It was green, and the consistency of soft clay. Lagertha felt a pleasant burning sensation in her hands, and she looked down shocked as the skin fused together and healed perfectly into the shape of her hands.

"You had better show your gratitude." she said.

"Your highness…Danu…I do not deserve…" she started.

"Not to me, you idiot!" she said. "To her!"

"Airmed, my lady. I am a fool." she said. "Please accept my eternal gratitude for the blessing that you have bestowed upon me today. From now on, I will be your humble and obedient servant."

"You are keeping the one on your neck." she said. "As a reminder of this discussion."

Airmed looked at Lagertha in dismay. She hadn't noticed the cut beneath her chin. It looked like it could be serious.

"Is that really necessary, my lady?" she asked. "After all, I am sure that Lagertha has learned her lesson. I have plenty of potion."

"Let us make an agreement, Airmed." she said calmly. "I will not advise you on how to heal, and you will not tell me how to deal with my subjects."

Her eyes flashed red again. Airmed went pale.

"Of course, your highness." she said.

Airmed stood there nervously looking at Lagertha's neck. She really felt the need to do something, yet she didn't dare cross Danu. She was the most powerful goddess in the universe. And those burning eyes! It was enough to frighten the stones, water, and air.

"Well?" she asked.

"Your highness?" asked Airmed.

"*BE GONE!*" she said.

Airmed disappeared immediately without a word.

"I have not yet decided if I will allow you to live. Are you ready to work?"

"Y-Yes your highness." she said.

"The only reason that I allowed Airmed to heal you is that you are going on the raids soon." she said. "I would have much preferred to let you suffer. Now, try to stop me as you did with Gersemi."

Danu turned and walked the other way. Lagertha concentrated on space and time, and arrived in Danu's path. At least she thought she did. She felt the blade resting on her shoulder, the edge pressed against her neck. Danu was standing behind her.

"You are dead." said Danu.

"Yes, your highness." she said. "How did you do that?"

"I simply countered your move." she said. "While you were travelling, I was also travelling."

"But how will this ever become a problem, your highness?" she asked. "I will not be fighting with those who may travel."

"That is your first mistake, child." she said. "You think that you live in a bubble. There is so much magic in this world that you are not aware of. You will learn. Time travel is elementary to many people. It really is a very rudimentary trick. Surely you do not think that you are the only person who can do this?"

"A week ago I did not think that *anyone* could do this." she said. "*Your highness.*"

She had almost forgotten how she wished to be addressed.

"This is not a game, *princess*." she said. "If you die, you die. You will leave a beautiful corpse, but that will be your only consolation. You will still be dead. You are of no use to the gods if you are dead."

"If so many people can do this, why have I never seen it before?" she asked.

Danu's eyes flashed red.

"*Your highness?*" she said nervously.

"You have not seen it because you have not opened your eyes." she said. "Like most humans, you cannot see beyond your own desires. I will teach you how. You will listen to me. You will learn to see beyond the end of your own nose. Try again."

She swiftly turned and walked in the other direction.

Lagertha focused on space and time and arrived at the place she wanted to be. She took extra care to think about what Danu was doing as she traveled. She tried to land behind her, anticipating that she would try the same trick as the last time and make the adjustment. She felt the blade on her neck again.

"It is simply too easy." said Danu. "You are dead…again."

"Yes, your highness." she said. "I tried to anticipate what you were doing this time."

"I know." she said. "That is why we are facing in the opposite direction. I knew that you would try to alter your move, and I countered it again. It is good that you were thinking ahead, but you must do better. You will practice this whenever the opportunity presents itself. Even in your day to day life. That is the only way you will learn. You will *not* involve outsiders as you did with Brunhilda."

"Yes, your highness." she said.

She had never called anyone 'your highness' in her life. Growing up, she always had servants and other underlings that called her 'my lady', which was the highest form of respect afforded anyone who was not a King or Queen. But what could she do? It wasn't like she could leave Danu at this juncture. And the gods, Odin in particular wanted her to work with Danu. It was simply something that she needed to get used to.

"I am going to walk into the forest." she said. "You will try again, in 5 minutes time. If my sword lands on your neck again, it is very likely that I will use it."

She turned and walked away.

It's a good thing that there's no pressure, she thought. How would she do this? The seconds were ticking away, she needed to act fast.

But wait a minute. Time was no longer an issue. She could go around it. She was free to go anytime that she pleased. She concentrated and travelled 15 minutes into the past.

She found a clearing where she figured that Danu would walk into. She waited patiently. A half hour had passed, and she still wasn't there. Somehow she had failed again.

Suddenly she heard her voice. It was coming from directly overhead. She looked up, and Danu was hovering over her.

"That was better." she said. "You used your brain and actually made a plan. We will meet back here again in 3 days. I expect progress."

With that she was gone.

Lagertha had an idea. She would go back in time again and meet her anyway. She would never expect that. She concentrated and arrived 3 minutes before Danu was due.

"I'm still here." she said.

Lagertha looked up, and Danu was hovering as before.

"But you are learning." she said. "You are starting to understand the nature of time. You will never outsmart me."

"Yes, your highness." she said.

"Go home." she said. "Keep practicing. We have very little time."

She flew straight up into the heavens, gone until their next meeting.

11

She was gliding up to the docks in Kattegat, as the sun was high in the western sky over Denmark. She tied off her boat and headed into town. As she approached the tent, there was the distinct odor of patchouli in the air. At least she's here, she thought. She walked into the tent.

"I've been expecting you." she said. "Sit."

"It seems that you are always expecting me." she said.

"No, child, I only expect you when the time for your arrival is eminent." she said. "Your step mothers are very suspicious of you now. You should not have involved Brunhilda. You must be careful when you travel, and *never* take someone with you as you did with her."

"I don't think you understand just how stupid she is." said Lagertha. "Trust me, she has no idea what happened."

"But Ama is *not* stupid." she said. "Did you not know that the two of them are lovers? The first thing she did was tell Ama. After that, they both confronted your father. Lucky for you, he has smoothed it all over. If not, Brunhilda and Ama would know too much. As it stands, they are both in a state of confusion over the whole ordeal. Ama is of a mind to figure it out. You must make sure that she doesn't."

"I know, Danu told me. Loose ends." she said. "Wait, did you say that Ama and Brun are *lovers*?"

This was news to Lagertha. She had no idea.

"Is it so surprising?" she asked. "They have been living together for 25 years."

"How do you know?" she asked.

"As I told you before, child, I am a seer." she said. "I see things. Whether I want to or not."

"Of course." she said. "I forgot who I was talking to for a moment."

"You forget things too often." she said. "You must change that. You must use your brain. You must think more…about everything. Before it did not matter. Now you are beyond human. You have been given a great gift, do not squander it."

"Yes, your highness." she said out of reflex. Disa was acting so bossy that she automatically called her 'your highness'.

"I am *not* anyone's highness." she said. "Save the deference for Danu, it is not required here. Is there something specific that you need my help with?"

"You're the seer, why don't you tell me?" she asked.

It felt good to be able to speak freely again. All that bowing and scraping with Danu had gotten on her nerves. Danu would kill her if she didn't show the utmost humility. She may kill her anyway. She had told her that she hadn't decided yet if she would let her live.

"Do not play games with me, child." she said. "Speak plainly. I have no time for this foolishness."

I guess I should just get to it, she thought. The problem is that she's so tight with Danu. Word of this conversation could *never* get back to her.

"She almost killed me the last time." she said. "Simply for speaking to her as I would anyone else. She cut me."

"From what I understand, the worst of your injuries were self-inflicted." she said. "And she called Airmed to heal you."

"I was fighting for my life!" she said. "I did what I had to do! I have never feared *anything* until I met her."

"You would be wise to remember that fear." she said. "Danu is not someone to be taken lightly. She is the most powerful goddess in the universe. *All* of us fear her. She will kill you without a second thought. The Norse gods answer to her. She is Odin's mother. Nobody would dare to question her, and she will not have any repercussions no matter what she does. You are in too deep now, child. There is no turning back."

The reality finally set in for Lagertha. This was not a game. If she didn't cooperate, she would be dead. How did she get herself into this?

It was so exciting at first, after she met Idun. And she thought that she had done so well with Gersemi. What a fool she was! Looking at it objectively for the first time, she saw that she had accomplished nothing. Gersemi was never a threat. She couldn't have picked an easier target.

She hadn't talked to daddy since the incident. That would not be a pleasant conversation. Disa was right. She needed to think things through more.

"Can I ask you a favor?" she said. "Don't tell Danu about this conversation?"

"Nothing that transpires in this tent is ever divulged to another party." she said. "But you forget who we speak of. If you do not think that Danu knows everything you say and think, you are deceiving yourself. We all walk lightly around her. Remember your manners. Your life may depend on it."

She held out her left hand.

"Really?" she asked. "We're done?"

"I am expecting another client." she said.

She snapped her fingers and held out her hand expectantly.

Lagertha sighed and licked it. She counted out 6 silver pieces and handed them to Disa.

Just then Gardi walked in. They exchanged puzzled looks.

"Father and daughter together." said Disa. "I have been expecting you. You would like to have a word in private with Lagertha before we begin."

She lifted a flap on the wall of the tent and disappeared into a hidden doorway, presumably into another room.

"That was creepy." said Lagertha. "Actually this whole situation is a little awkward."

"I didn't expect to find you here." he said.

"Do you think I expected to see you walk through the door?" she asked. "What do you need to talk to me about, daddy?"

"It's about Brun." he said.

"I've already been told." she said. "It was stupid of me to involve her."

"Yes." he said. "I had to do some pretty slick dancing to explain that. I'm not sure that they're off the scent. I mean, Brun has probably let it go by now, but Ama is a different story. You must be more careful. And what's the deal with the wolves?"

"She told you about that?" she asked. "Why would she do that?"

"You're forgetting who we're talking about." he said. "Why *wouldn't* she? Why are you so close to the wolves? When did this happen? Why didn't I know about it?"

"There are many things that you don't know about me daddy." she said. "Don't you remember how young I was when I started hunting? Do you think I did it all by myself?"

"When did it start?" he asked.

"I guess when I was around 7 or 8." she said. "I was walking in the forest one day and I encountered a wolf. His name was Broderic. I can't explain it, but we began to communicate. Not like you and I are now, but on a telepathic level. Gradually I met to the rest of the pack. I was so young that I was scared to tell you about it. As time went by, I thought it would be better if I kept it a secret. They taught me many things over the years. They have been my dear friends ever since."

""You certainly are full of surprises Lagertha." he said.

She decided that she had come this far, she may as well tell him the rest. She had always been curious, and he was the only one that could give her the answers...if he was willing to tell. She could usually get him to talk.

"Broderic told me that I was destined to work with the gods, like my sister." she said. "My only sisters are Magnilda, Siv, and Nanna. None of them are involved with the gods. Broderic told me that I would understand when the time comes. Do I have another sister?"

Gardi looked from side to side briefly, then directly into her eyes. What should he say?

Just then Disa came back.

"I must speak with your father now." she said.

Lagertha looked at her. The wolves. *She* knew them as well. *They raised her.* Could it be her? No way, she was too old. But then daddy *has* been around for a long time.

She didn't always understand what Broderic was saying. She was sure that he said her *sister*, but sometimes things got lost in the translation with him. He considered everyone in the pack to be his brothers and sisters, even if they had different mothers. He had to know that it was different for humans. He wasn't stupid. She had picked up signals in conversation with him that confirmed that he knew the difference. Why would he say sister?

"Okay." she said. "We will continue this conversation later?"

Gardi was visibly relieved. Looking at him, Lagertha was even more suspicious. It seemed that he didn't want to talk about it. Disa had rescued him in the nick of time.

"Absolutely." he said. "Shall we stay in the city for the night?"

"No, I want to get back to Skagen to see Arve." she said. "I'll find you."

"Have a safe trip." he said.

She walked out of the tent. She lingered for a moment hoping to catch some of the conversation.

"That was close." he said.

"Such questions are bound to come up." she said. "The important thing is how we handle them. She must never know that I am your daughter."

Lagertha stumbled back a couple of steps in disbelief. Had she just heard that?

Asgard

"How is she doing?" asked Odin. "Will she be ready?"

"Why do you ask questions that you already know the answers to, my son?" replied Danu.

"Why must you answer a question with a question?" he asked. "You are here as a courtesy."

Her blazed red. She took a moment before answering.

He certainly had a high opinion of himself. He grew more arrogant every day. She would really love to put him in his place, but that would rupture the delicate peace.

Strangely, in spite of her personality, she did not wish to go to war. When the gods battle, everyone loses.

Still, I need to remind him who is in charge. The other gods eyed her nervously.

"Had I not decided to birth you more than 2000 years ago, you would not exist." she said coolly. "I think that is a much greater courtesy than being included in your little club. I brought you into this world, and I can just as easily show you the exit. Do not test me Odin. You will fail."

Thor tightened his grip on his hammer, while the other gods shrank back and tried to look as small as possible. They all knew her power, even Thor. They knew that she could destroy all of them without a second thought.

"My apologies, your highness, I meant no disrespect." he said. "Of course I have been watching her progress, I merely thought that you are the best judge of how she is doing. You are far more powerful and perceptive than me, and I would never think that my opinion counts for anything where you are concerned."

Her eyes returned to normal. Thor relaxed his grip. It was in his nature to fight no matter what the odds. His father's words had snapped him back to reality. The other gods breathed a sigh of relief that their father had diffused the situation.

"I have not yet decided if I will let her live." she said. "She is very disrespectful."

Thor tightened his grip again. There was no way he was going to let this bitch destroy their plans…*his plans*. Odin held up his hand in Thor's general direction. He loosened his grip again.

"With respect, your highness, as you know, I have been watching." he said. "She is no different from any other human. This is all new to her. Less than a month ago, she had never met a goddess. We sometimes forget that it is a lot to take in. She *has* tried to address you with respect. We all know that she has a healthy fear of you, as we all do. Is her progress so inadequate that we should give up on her now?"

"That will be my decision." she said. "She is learning. She must do better."

"Yes, your highness." he said.

He knew that the conversation was over and he could say no more. He had already upset her with his flippant remark. Best to live to fight another day.

"Does anybody have anything else to add?" he asked.

They all looked around anxiously, hoping to stay invisible.

"I just…" Thor started.

Odin cut him off.

"You and I will speak later." he said. "You have nothing to say now, son."

"Remember your place, Odin." said Danu. "You and your people will show me the respect that I deserve."

She looked directly at Thor as her eyes flashed red once again. He glared back at her, but said nothing.

* * *

Baldur was sitting by the water. He was thinking about his brother...not Leif, Sveyn, Kol, or Bjørn, but Freki. He had always regretted how he treated Freki when they were younger. He wondered how he was doing now.

In many ways, he felt closer to Freki than his blood brothers. They were so close in age, yet so different. He still felt a strong bond with him. They had grown up together.

He never disliked him, he just felt that he was timid when it came to fighting. Sure, when he fought he was usually successful, but he didn't *want* to fight. It just seemed like a foreign concept to him. Why wouldn't he want to fight? It was in their blood. All one had to do is to look at their father, and it should be obvious that *all* of his sons should be warriors.

Sometimes Baldur envied him his passive attitude. He never seemed to get upset about anything. Baldur was the opposite. He had inherited his mother's temper. It took almost nothing to set him off. It had gotten him in trouble on several occasions.

Not Freki. He was cool as ice in every situation. He would always calmly find the correct solution and act on it. He was smart, Baldur envied him that too. As a result of his intelligence, father depended on his advice and told him things that he never would have told Baldur. Only Freki was involved in those conversations...the planning and execution. And he was damned good at it!

The water was as smooth as a sheet of ice. He tossed a stone out there and watched the ripples smoothly roll across the surface of the water in every direction. He got up and started walking home.

When we get to England and pop goes to visit him, I'll come along, he thought. He didn't have any illusions that he would give him some kind of tearful apology, that wasn't his style. He would try to make peace though.

Pop had told him that Alfdis had converted to the false religion. That had to be tough. He hoped that Freki was staying strong. Certainly he was too smart to believe all that hype.

One thing Baldur had never done was worry about Freki. He knew that his brother could take care of himself no matter what.

Still it bothered him. He knew that there was little he could do to help him. The problem was that Freki had never *needed* his help. There were the occasional times when he came to his defense in battle, but he always figured that Freki didn't really need him for that either. He was so smart that he usually found a way to neutralize his opponent that Baldur never would have thought of. He worried about Freki's relationship with the gods. How would he ever make it to Valhalla?

He walked in the door and Gytha was waiting for him. She gave him that smile that always made his heart melt. After almost 30 years of marriage, he still loved with her as much as the day they met.

She was a natural beauty, and she still looked good at 49. He was sure that she was getting grey like him, but she was a blonde, and it blended in. His hair was getting more salt than pepper every day.

She held a finger to her lips.

"She's sleeping, finally!" she whispered.

"Is she feeling better?" he whispered back.

She shook her head.

"She's so hard headed." she replied. "Like you!"

He feigned shock.

"Me? Hard headed?" he said.

"SHHHH! You'll wake her!" said Gytha. "Let's go outside."

They walked out towards the forest.

"What's troubling you, elsker?" she asked.

She could always tell. Even when they were younger, she always knew when something was wrong. It was pointless to try to evade the issue. She was like a wolf when she got a hold of something. She wouldn't let go until it was dead.

"How do you always know?" he asked.

"You are a part of me." she said quietly. "I am a part of you. When you hurt I hurt. Now what is it?"

"I'm worried about Freki." he said. "Pop says that Alfdis has converted to the false religion."

"And what does that have to do with Freki?" she asked.

He rolled his eyes.

"Isn't it obvious?" he asked. "She's his wife. She's always had influence over him. I'm worried about his afterlife."

"Why the sudden concern for your long lost brother?" she asked. "Forgive me, but I didn't think you cared."

"Of course I do!" he said. "Most people don't know it, or just assume different, but I care very much for him. We didn't always see eye to eye when we were younger, but I've mellowed with age."

"You don't have to worry about Alfdis." she said. "They won't be together for much longer."

"Really?" he asked. "Have you seen this?"

"Yes. It's all but over." she said.

She hesitated to tell him the rest. She was worried about Freki too. He had no religion at all now. She knew that Freki was smart. Sometimes too smart for his own good.

She couldn't burden Baldur with this information so close to the voyage. She worried about him too much as it was, even though she knew that he could take care of himself very well.

After all these years, she still had not gotten over worrying about him while he was on the raids. She wasn't worried about his fidelity, she knew that he took other lovers while he was away. She was worried about his safety.

She figured he would find out soon enough. She had seen him meeting with Freki while they were in England. It wasn't clear what the results of the meeting with Freki were…yet. She would know before Baldur knew.

"It certainly is nice to know someone with inside information." he said. "Why are they splitting?"

"There are a number of reasons." she said. "Her new faith is the key issue, though. She wants to have the marriage annulled and get remarried as Christians. Freki won't do it."

"It must be nice to know the future." he said.

"I know something else." she said.

"And what is that?" he asked.

"My husband is going to make love to me." she said. "Right out here in the forest like we used to do as teenagers."

"You're very perceptive." he said.

"That remains to be seen." she said. "In order to get your reward, you'll have to catch me first."

"You think I can't?" he asked.

"Oh, I'm counting on it." she said.

She started giggling and took off. He was hot on her trail, but she didn't make it easy. He chased her for a half mile before he caught her. She had left a trail of clothing behind her, and when he got there she was taking off her boots.

"You know I *let* you catch me." she said.

He looked into her eyes.

"I was counting on it." he said.

* * *

As he cast off from the dock in Kattegat, the sun was setting over Denmark. There was only a tiny sliver on the horizon, providing just enough light to get out of the harbor. He kept the coast on his left as he sailed north.

He didn't know what to think of his encounter with Lagertha. Idun had sent her to Disa, but it was still a shock to see her there. What if she found out? They had a strong connection. They were both friends to the wolves. The *same* wolves. What if one of the wolves told her?

He couldn't think about it. Why had Idun sent her to Disa? She was already working with Danu, who better to help her with the adjustment?

This was all just difficult to comprehend. His daughter, *Brenda's* daughter, now had almost as much power as he did. Perhaps more. He couldn't travel through time, not that he ever wanted to. Most of the time, he didn't even want to be immortal.

He thought back to that fateful hunting trip 54 years ago. If he had never met Idun, he would be an ordinary man. Hell, he would probably be dead by now. It seemed to be a running theme in his thoughts, as well as his dreams. What if he had never met Idun?

It was far too late for regrets now. It was too late the moment that he bit into that apple.

Would he have married Astrid? Brenda? Would he have met his father's killer? Would he have known him if he had?

He glided into the dock at Skagen and tied off the boat. He started walking towards the hall.

A woman approached him and started walking alongside. She was wearing a loose fitting cloak with a hood that hid her face. He didn't know why, but he felt comfortable walking with her. She had a familiar quality, he felt that he knew her already without speaking.

"It's been a long time." she said quietly.

He examined her closely again. The voice even seemed familiar.

"Do we know each other?" he asked.

"Intimately." she replied. "I'll forgive you. It's been more than 50 years. But we must speak."

She lifted both hands to the hood and slowly withdrew it from her face. She flashed him a pretty smile. He couldn't believe his eyes. She hadn't aged a minute. She was supposed to be dead, but then again so was her daughter.

"Margaret?" he asked.

12

After everything that had happened in the last few weeks, he wasn't surprised. He had been beyond surprise for a long time. Disa was a surprise, but after she explained it to him it made sense...still, Margaret?

Yes, elsker, it is me." she said.

"You haven't aged." he said.

"Neither have you." she quipped.

"I guess that's true." he said. "Although I have lived these past 53 years, something tells me that you haven't."

"I am the same woman that you met back in England." she said. "I travel as your daughters Lagertha and Disa do."

"I don't believe that you were *ever* the same woman I met in England." he said.

"I will admit that I was deceitful." she said. "We both know now that it was necessary. You were meant for a higher purpose. We both worship the same gods, we just have different names for them. I needed to connect with you back then. For Lagertha's sake. It was my purpose in life."

"For Lagertha's sake?" he asked. "And how did you know about Lagertha 26 years before she was born?"

"She is one of the keys to our mission." she said. "This was all planned…"

"Yes, I know, thousands of years ago." he finished. "I thought that Brenda killed you for sure."

"A time traveler never really dies." she said quietly. "We can skip ahead or go back any time we want. So you see, we have the power to do things over if we don't like the outcome."

"That's convenient." he said.

"Do you remember the tea I used to make you?" she asked. "After Disa was born? Every morning and every night. I made sure that you drank all of it. Brenda was so jealous."

"Of course." he said. "I loved that tea. After you were gone, Brenda tried to figure out how to make it, but she never got it right."

"It was an ancient recipe from Arianrhod, a goddess who oversees reincarnation amongst other things." she said. "We wanted to give your only daughter with Brenda the spirit of some of our goddesses…including Danu. That is why it was vital that you and I connect. Do you see how important Lagertha is now?"

"I knew that she was different as soon as Idun started talking about her." he said.

"It was fated." she said.

"So what happened? With Brenda?" he asked.

"She took me for a walk in the forest." she said. "I thought her walks in the forest were common knowledge."

"And you went willingly?" he asked.

"It was fated." she said. "But you see I'm ok, don't you?"

"How is that possible?" he asked. "If she killed you, how could you travel back in time?"

"Simple. I played dead. It was rather convincing, since I wasn't technically there at the time." she said. "In my mind, I was back in Eire."

"The land across the sea that Disa spoke of." he said. "How did you do that?"

"A little trick my mother taught me." she said.

"Danu?" he asked.

"Who else?" she said.

"You will have to be patient with me, Margaret, although I have been acquainted with the gods for some time now, yours are new to me." he said. "I know a little about Danu, but my daughter knows more."

"*Two* of your daughters do." she corrected.

"I'm still trying to get used to *that*." he said. "Why won't she let me introduce her to the family? She already knows Lagertha. And how fair that to her? She's talking to her *sister* in the guise of a seer!"

"She may have a biased opinion of your family, particularly those associated with Brenda." she said. "Disa is very particular. She doesn't have any friends…or family besides us."

"We all know that Brenda was crazy." he said. "Her children are a little rough around the edges as well, and Lagertha is by far the most like her. If she's so scared, why is she working with Lagertha?"

"You misunderstand me, husband." she said. "I never said that Disa was scared. That girl has never been scared of anything in her life. She prefers to keep her life simple, and extended family complicates things."

"Did I miss something? Are we married?" he asked. "Because my wives would have something to say about that."

"Sweet Gardi, we are married in every way before the gods." she said. "We were married long before you even thought of Brunhilda and Ama. We will still be married long after they are gone. I've already outlived two of your wives…even the one who killed me."

He laughed at the irony of what she said.

"Do you even hear what you're saying?" he asked.

"The moment you saw me in Lindisfarne, you were mine." she said. "I already knew that Astrid was dead, and that Brenda would kill me. It didn't matter. I did what I did out of love."

They were almost back at the hall, on a grassy plain near the forest. The moon was full, and it bathed the whole scene in an eerie blue light.

"You're tired. We will speak again tomorrow." she said.

She wrapped her arms around his neck and leaned in, pressing her body against his. She met his lips with hers and gave him a passionate kiss. He started to protest, but immediately gave in, and returned her affection with a zeal he wasn't aware that he had.

"I've missed you." she said.

"How do I know that?" he asked. "For me it's been 53 years. For you, it could have been as little as a few minutes."

"Oh, elsker, being apart from you for only a moment is an eternity to me." she said. "I will find you tomorrow."

With that, she sauntered into the forest and disappeared.

He was blown away. He was prepared to resist her, but as soon as she touched him, he fell apart.

* * *

She had been watching him since he landed. She had to get to the bottom of this.

She knew he could keep a secret, she had heard the stories about the time shortly after he became immortal. But still, Disa? She knew that he hadn't been seeing her for very long…unless he was doing so in private. That was entirely possible. His wives couldn't even get information out of him if he didn't want to give it up.

She was about to walk up to him when a mysterious woman got there first. Out of curiosity she fell back and followed them.

Who was that woman he was talking to? He seemed to know her pretty well. Her body language told Lagertha that she knew him intimately. When she lowered her hood, for a split second he registered a slight shock, then as usual he was cool and composed.

He better be careful, they're getting pretty close to the hall, and if one of his wives sees him, he'll be in big trouble. Who was she kidding? He wouldn't be in trouble. He had those two wrapped around his little finger.

They're probably too busy with each other anyway, she thought. She had an inward chuckle at the thought. Did he know about *that*?

They had stopped at the edge of the forest, about a hundred yards away from the hall. It looked like they were saying their goodbyes, when she leaned into him and gave him a kiss on the mouth that he willingly returned.

She gasped and raised her hand to her mouth. What is daddy doing? Who *is* this woman? She casually walked into the forest and disappeared into the trees.

As soon as she was gone she headed straight for him.

"And who was that?" she demanded.

He looked at her shocked for a second, then immediately confident.

"Lagertha! You scared me!" he said.

"Come off it, daddy, you don't scare!" she said. "Now who was that woman?"

"She's an old friend." he said.

"She didn't look that old to me." she said. "As a matter of fact, I would say she's younger than *I am*!"

"Technically, so am I." he said.

"Don't play semantic games, daddy." she said. "Just tell me who she is!"

"You wouldn't believe me if I told you." he said.

"Okay, let's get back to her in a minute." she said. "When were you going to tell me about Disa?"

"What about Disa?" he asked. "I thought that you knew I was seeing her."

Does she know? How could she? Did Disa tell her? No, not her, it's impossible. She doesn't want to know the family, she made that clear from the start.

"Fine. I know the truth. If you don't want to tell me, I'll ask her about it." she said.

She does know. How?

"Honestly, I'd rather talk about the woman." he said, hoping for the best.

"Do you have any other children that I don't know about?" she asked.

I suppose a little damage control is in order, he thought. I'll try to get her not to mention this to Disa. Disa! She probably already knows.

"I didn't even know she was alive until a couple of weeks ago." he said. "I was sure that she was dead."

He thought about telling her who 'killed' her, but that would only make things worse.

"So you just randomly showed up at her tent and she told you?" she asked.

"No, Idun sent me to her, same as you." he said. "Of course Idun knew who she was sending me to. She played a trick on me."

"So why did Idun send me?" she asked.

"I was wondering that myself." he said. "Disa has a lot of experience with the powers you're using now. You need all the help you can get."

"I guess that makes sense." she said. "But why didn't you tell me about it immediately? Don't you think that I would want to know?"

"She doesn't want anyone to know." he said. "I wanted to bring her back here to meet everyone, but she refused. You probably shouldn't let on that you know."

"Are you forgetting who we're talking about here, daddy?" she asked. "She probably knew that I would find out before it happened."

"The thought had crossed my mind." he said. "And since you mentioned it, how *did* you find out?"

She went blank momentarily. What should I say?

"It doesn't matter how I know." she said. "I just do. And neither my sister nor my father told me."

"It wasn't because I didn't want to." he said. "She insisted. While we're on the subject, none of your siblings can know about this either."

"I can't keep a secret like you, daddy." she said.

"You must keep this one." he said. "I promised her."

"I'll do my best, daddy." she said. "Speaking of secrets, who is that woman?"

"That was Margaret." he said. "Disa's mother."

* * *

He was lying in bed next to her exhausted. Suddenly a black and white cat crawled up and curled up in a ball and laid on her stomach.

The cat glared at him and looked at her disapprovingly. Does this cat know that I used to sacrifice animals?

"I'm okay now kitty." he said with a smile. "I gave all that up years ago."

Annabel stirred and woke up.

"I see you've met Huckleberry." she said.

"I don't think he likes me." said Freki.

"Oh, don't mind him." she said. "He's very protective and jealous. He'll get used to you in time."

"I guess I'm lucky he's not bigger." he said. "Considering what we just did."

"Yeah, you are." said a strange voice. "If I was half your size, I'd kick your ass. You should remember that I can still do damage with these."

Huckleberry was holding up his paw with the claws extended.

Freki shook his head in an effort to clear it. Did that cat just talk to me?

"Did you hear that?!" he asked.

"What?" she asked. "Oh, him. Don't worry about that, he purrs really loud. I tried to measure his heartbeat once, but I couldn't get a read on it, he's too loud."

"No, I could swear he just talked to me." he said.

"How much wine did you have at the party?" she asked. "He's a cat, he can't talk. Not our language anyway. He usually doesn't even have much to say in his own language."

Suddenly Freki felt very stupid.

"This is between us." said Huckleberry. "Don't get her involved. You're the only one I've ever met that understands me. Let's keep it that way. I can barely get this one to shut up as it is."

He nodded his head in the general direction of Annabel.

"Maybe I did have too much to drink." he said.

"No question about it, you jackass." he said. "But this is me talking, not the wine. She likes you, so I guess I'll give you a chance. Pet me across my back a couple of times so I can save face. I don't want to appear weak."

He did as he was told.

Huck got up and started rubbing his face against Freki's hand.

"This doesn't mean I like you." he said. "It's all a show for her. We will discuss this some other time. I think you should go now."

"What a sweetheart!" she cried. "See? He *does* like you! I've never seen him so friendly with a stranger!"

"I guess it worked." said Freki.

"Guess what worked?" she asked.

"Nothing...never mind." he said.

"You were leaving?" said Huck.

The cat was glaring at him again, careful not to let Annabel see.

"I really don't want to, but I have to go." he said. "Alfdis is probably going crazy already. I should try to find some fish before I go home. I told her that I was going fishing. I had a great time."

"Will I see you again?" she asked.

"I don't see why not." he said.

"Well, you know where I live." she said. "I had a great time too, Freki. You're a very interesting man. I would love to see you again."

"I'll be in touch." he said.

As he turned to leave he heard Huck again.

"I'm not sure about you yet, but still, I don't like to see a man in trouble with his woman." he said "Go to the river and take your shirt off and wade out. Hold it in the water and talk to the fish as you have talked to me. They will swim up to you and you can catch them with your shirt. If you want to make a good impression on me, bring me one the next time you come over. You will meet others on your way home."

"Thanks." he said.

"For what?" she asked.

"For being so understanding." he said. "You're easy to like."

"That's so sweet!" she said. "I meant what I said Freki. I want you to come back and see me."

"I will." he said.

If for no other reason than to figure out if I'm crazy, he thought. He walked out the door.

The dialogue with the cat stunned him. Did that really happen? No, there was no scientific explanation, it couldn't have. She was probably right, he had too much to drink.

He started the walk home. The sun was just rising in the east, but it wasn't quite light yet. He was walking on a path through the forest, not far from the river.

Should he try the thing with the fish? Like Huck said? He couldn't believe that he was even thinking it! *That cat did not talk to me! His lips weren't even moving!* But would an animal's lips move? *He doesn't even have lips!* Get a hold of yourself!

Maybe they put something in the wine at the party. Yes! That's the explanation. Someone slipped a hallucinogen in my drink! It was probably that Edward! I really embarrassed him with the whole heliocentric thing. He was somewhat relieved that he had apparently figured it out. Cats talking to people! What was he thinking!

He heard a weak cry in the forest. Then he started hearing words.

"Don't come any closer! I can't run yet, I can barely walk!" said the squeaky voice.

He looked in the direction of the voice, but he didn't see anything. He heard a louder more confident voice now.

"Stay away from her!" it said.

He looked closer and saw a large doe standing proudly in front of a tiny fawn.

"I'm not trying to hurt you." he said. "I'm just walking home."

"Just keep your distance, we don't want any trouble." said the doe.

He couldn't believe that he was speaking to the animal, and what was even stranger, it understood him and answered back.

"Look. It's been a long night." he said. "I'm not even sure if we're talking now. I mean you no harm."

"Then just keep walking." it said.

That must have been a very powerful hallucinogen, he thought. It's still affecting my consciousness almost 12 hours later. Suddenly a butterfly flew past him.

"You must follow me, Freki." it said.

What the hell is going on? He started after the butterfly, but he was having a hard time keeping up. It slowed down and doubled back to him.

"Try to keep up, it's not much further." it said.

"Remember that I cannot fly." he said. "I don't even know why I'm talking to you, this doesn't make any sense."

"It will momentarily." said the butterfly. "Who knows? Maybe it won't. You've become so rigid that you may not be able to understand. You used to believe, I'm sure that's what she's counting on."

"Who?" he asked.

The butterfly swooped around a large bush into a clearing. There was a beautiful red haired woman sitting cross-legged in the shade, stroking the fawn from before between the ears. It was shaking, and looked at Freki with concern.

"It's okay young one." said the woman. "He will not hurt you. This one is my son."

Freki looked at her confused.

"Your son?" he asked.

"Yes." she replied. "There is a reason that I sent the butterfly for you. It is a symbol of transformation. You are not losing your mind, you are simply regaining a part of it that you have abandoned. My name is Astrid, and I am your mother."

13

"Disa's Mother?" she asked. "It can't be! She looks younger than me! What are you playing at, daddy?"

"She's a traveler. Like you." he said. "She's my age...my true age. She came here from the time when Disa was born."

"So what is she doing here?" she asked.

"I don't know." he said. "She said she needs to talk to me. I didn't get around to asking her why."

"From what I could tell, you were too busy kissing her!" she said. "You better hope your wives didn't see that!"

"It's complicated." he said.

"We've got company." said Lagertha.

She nodded towards the water. There were 3 boats approaching. They were definitely Viking, but Gardi didn't recognize them. That didn't really mean anything, there were many Viking boats that came to Skagen since Gardi lived here.

Just then, Baldur and some other men walked up. Gardi was too far away to be able to tell who was on the ships.

"Can you tell who it is?" asked Gardi.

"I was on the shore when they came into view." he said. "It's Jarl Erik of Götaland. The last I heard, he was in England."

Gardi remembered a meeting with the Jarl in early March. He wanted to go to England early, because he was concerned about what he had heard about King Guðrum. He had gotten careless and cocky with King Alfred, and Erik wanted to make sure that Guðrum didn't squander their gains in the west.

He wanted to leave immediately, and try to control the situation.

Guðrum was actually doing very well, having his way with Alfred, and taking new territory with impunity. Erik knew that every man had pride, and there was nothing more dangerous than a man who was being made a fool of.

He knew Guðrum well, and he knew that he would have no problem twisting the knife, in fact he would enjoy it.

He also knew Alfred, and sooner or later he would turn the tables. Gardi told him to go, and try to rein him in.

The boats glided into the docks and Erik jumped onto the dock.

"What's going on over there?" asked Gardi.

"He was doing fine for a long time." said Erik. "Then he got careless."

"How bad is it?" he asked.

"Alfred has him cornered." he said. "He's just waiting him out now. It might be over by the time we get back. I had to come and get you. We have to try."

"We'll leave at first light." said Gardi. "Baldur. Get your crew together. Get the word out to everyone. Lagertha, you too. Get your crew together. I don't know if we can make a difference, but we have to try."

"What do you think, Erik?"

"Nobody likes the man who brings bad news." he said. "It doesn't look good. He's playing it badly. We may lose Wessex."

Asgard

"It is all but over now." said Odin. "That idiot let them get the upper hand. Why did we trust Guðrum? They have retreated to Chippenham. The West Saxons have blocked all the food and supplies for miles. They have them surrounded. They have only to wait them out now."

"But he is on his way?" asked Thor. "And Lagertha? All of his people?"

"How can you be so simple?" asked Loki. "You do know that it takes time to cross the sea, do you not? Guðrum fucked us *all* on this! He is doomed! Mark my words, he will surrender before Gardi gets halfway there."

"Calm down." said Idun. "This is why we have Gardi. Make no mistake, we will take a substantial loss, but Gardi is still out there. He makes people believe simply by existing."

"Idun is right, but so is Loki." said Danu. "Having Gardi will help, and I have other plans for his little girl. We all know that Guðrum will surrender as soon as he gets a little hungry. There is no telling what will happen after that. He has the spine of a jellyfish."

Danu had begun regularly attending the meetings of the gods in Asgard. No one dared to challenge her. If she felt that one of them was getting brave, she flashed her eyes red.

"I do not want to admit defeat, yet it seems that I have no choice." said Odin. "How did we let this craven gain this much power?"

"It depends on who you ask." said Freyja. "According to some, it was fated thousands of years ago. I believe in fate, but come on, really?"

"We all knew that this moment was coming." said Danu. "It is *not* over. If it wasn't Guðrum, it would surely be someone else. If you do not believe in fate, that is just fine, princess. Guðrum is not the problem. We were *fated* for this a long time ago."

She glared at Freyja, and reflexively Freyja made herself as small as possible and broke whatever weak eye contact she had managed to muster.

"Is there nothing we can do?" asked Odin.

"Unfortunately, my son, all we can do is wait." said Danu. "Gardi will surely get there too late. We must do damage control, yet we do not know the damage. Do not expect a good outcome. It depends largely on how loyal Guðrum is. Make no mistake, this is not about him. This was fated. Even as gods, we cannot influence fate."

"I could go down there." said Thor. "I could solve the problem before the sun sets."

"Without reminding you how utterly inappropriate that would be, I will tell you that it is a waste of time." said Danu. "Even if you overpower Alfred, it will not end there. Do any of you understand how fate works? If we somehow escape this tragedy, something else will happen almost immediately. At this time in history, *this happens*. It was *always* meant to happen. Believe me, I know about time. So we can sit back and enjoy the show, or intervene and watch another show that might have the potential to be worse than this one."

"I understand completely, mother." said Odin.

He looked the other gods over with compassion.

"We must not interfere. She is right." he said. "There is another disaster waiting in the wings if this one fails. We still have Gardi, Lagertha, and whoever else my mother is working with. I am not privy to that information."

Danu scowled at him.

"If such information were relevant to you, my son, you would know it. That goes for all of you." she said.

Her eyes flashed red briefly.

"What I do is find solutions, which sometimes requires me to think creatively. Who I have working on this is my affair alone. Does anyone have anything else?" she asked.

They all looked at her with visible anxiety. Nobody said a word.

"Good. I didn't think so." she said. "This meeting is adjourned."

Odin looked at her in disbelief. He alone was supposed to adjourn the meetings.

"Did you have something else?" she asked.

Odin shook his head sadly. It was killing him to submit to her, but he was powerless to do anything about it.

"Very well." she said "Dismissed."

She quickly stood up, turned on her heel and left.

Dismissed! Now she was dismissing his gods as though they were children.

She was making things embarrassing for him. She was his mother technically, but he had always had a hard time earning her respect. It was always this way. He would be happy when she finally departed Scandinavia.

* * *

"My mother died in childbirth when I was born." he said. "Who are you really?"

"Why do you not believe me, Freki?" she asked. "When did you become so jaded?"

"The presence of my dead mother petting a fawn in the forest cannot be explained scientifically, therefore, it is not true." he said. "And what kind of twisted sense of humor do you have to pretend to be my mother? What do you take me for?"

"I take you for an intelligent man who has wandered off the true path." she said. "Did you know that your father is on his way?"

"Of course he is." he said. "He comes every year at about this time. You're forgetting about the stops in France, though. He won't be here for months."

"That is where you are wrong, Baldur." she said. "King Guðrum has been trapped. Your father is on the way to help. Sadly it will be too late."

"Baldur is my brother's name." he said.

"How silly of me!" she said. "You have always been Baldur to me. Brenda lied to your father and told him that I wanted to name you Freki after my father. It was my intention to honor your other grandfather by naming you after him. It matters little now, whatever your name is you are the same person. You are my son."

"Why should I believe anything you say?" he asked. "My mother is dead. Someone spiked my drink at a party I went to last night, that's all this is. It must have been some powerful stuff, because you wouldn't believe some of the things I've seen and heard. Why am I talking to you? You're not even here."

"This is not over, Freki." she said. "I'll let you go home to your wife now, but you and I are not finished. You feel disoriented because you have been gifted with the power of communication with animals. That was *not* a mistake. We are trying to lead you back to the true gods. Whether you like it or not, I will talk to you later."

"I don't believe in the gods anymore." He said quietly. "Such beliefs are irrational. I believe only in what I can see before my own eyes."

"If that is how it must be, then perhaps I must show you something the next time we meet." she said. "Go home and get some rest. See if your hallucinogen wears off by the time you wake up. I'll see you soon…"

"I predict that we never meet again." he said.

He turned quickly and made his way home.

* * *

They were underway, 2 weeks from Skagen with a brisk wind at their backs. He didn't have much hope of getting there in time.

Erik said the situation was dire, and Gardi believed him.

Guðrum was a bit of a fool at times too. Overconfident might be a better way of putting it, at least *that* was diplomatic. Gardi knew that the time for diplomacy was over.

He had accepted the fact that they would almost certainly lose a good chunk of England. He really hoped that the embarrassment would stop there. There was no telling what kind of concessions King Alfred would demand. The situation was completely out of their control.

He remembered how Idun had warned him about this. The ever present *fate*. How could a man go through his life with so little control? How was it possible that everything was determined by something as random as fate? Had they ever had a choice? He knew better than to argue the point. He had been hearing it since he was a small child.

He looked over at Lagertha. She raised an eyebrow, as if to remind him that she still wanted to get to the bottom of what she saw with Margaret. How would he explain *that*? Probably how he explained everything, He would say what he wanted to say about it, then that would be the end of it. He had a harder time doing that with Lagertha than almost anyone.

She reminded him *so* much of her mother. He still missed Brenda, as well as Astrid. Disa had hinted that Brenda was involved with Astrid's death, but he didn't know what to believe. Everyone he talked to said that she died because of the childbirth. At this point he didn't care, it was so long ago. Brenda would always be Brenda. He didn't put it past her. If she *did* do it, she hid it well. He tried everything he could think of to find out if she had done it, and she passed every test.

"Land!" cried the lookout.

Sure enough, a thin slice of shore was visible on the edge of the horizon. Gardi knew it well, it was the coast of Northumbria. From here they would head south and go inland at the Ouse River into Guðrum's kingdom, or whatever was left of it. Fate. He was going more out of honor and obligation than anything else. He didn't have any illusions that there would be some rosy outcome.

That fact wouldn't stop them from raiding a few villages along the way. He knew that there was very little he could do, so he figured that his crew deserved some reward for such a thankless mission.

"Prepare for battle!" he shouted. "We'll start with Lindisfarne."

The other boats started getting their swords and shields ready.

Lagertha had a wild grin on her face. This was her first chance to prove herself with her *own* crew. She forgot all about Margaret.

It came with the territory, having a legend for a father. There were always *something* a little strange going on.

If her father wanted Margaret around, those two bitches would fall in line. They had little choice. You marry an immortal, you have to put up with a lot of things, but the rewards are worth it.

She knew that neither Brun nor Ama would have it any other way. They had a good life.

The whole thing with Gersemi still pissed her off. Who did Brun think she was? She chuckled to herself at the reaction she got when she introduced her to Broderic. That skank didn't know *what* to think!.

Those two hid behind him every chance they got. Not so much Brunhilda, she had to admit that *she* was a bit of a badass, but that pathetic little Ama! She was *so* sneaky! Lagertha was smart, but Ama was smarter, and she knew it. It was entertaining to watch how she pushed Brun around without her even knowing it.

They would be ashore in a few hours, why was she thinking about her stepmothers? She had to get ready, she had to get her *crew* ready. Arve walked up.

"You ready for this?" he asked.

"Would it sound too cliché if I said I was born ready?" she asked.

"I honestly believe that it's true." he said.

She gave him a huge kiss.

"You always know just what to say." she said.

"With you it's usually easy to figure out." he said.

"Watch it!" she said. "You were doing pretty good there, don't fuck it up!"

He held his hands up in protest.

"I didn't mean any offense!" he said. "All I meant was that in addition to being beautiful, you're a hell of a warrior."

"Nice save." she said. "But I have my eye on you!"

"That's good to know." he said. "There is no possible way that I could look away from you."

She was happy with him. He was different. Not like Gunnar, but definitely as strong. It wasn't that he didn't take any shit from her, but he took just enough to show that her opinion mattered, but not enough to look weak. He was very well balanced.

He never said so, but he hinted that he was a little disturbed about what had happened to Gersemi. He wasn't upset enough to say anything, after all, he knew who he was getting involved with from the start.

The thing she liked was that she didn't scare him off. There were a lot of men that would have run for the hills after all that had happened, but Arve stayed. It proved to her that she was more than just a piece of ass to him. She had a good feeling about him. She hoped that it would work out for another reason too. She had missed her moon for the first time ever. Her mother had always told her she would know when it happened, so did Ama and Brun. She knew. Could she be a good mother?

Even though her mother was away a lot, she always knew that she loved her. Brenda always came to her defense, no matter how far out of line she was (and she realized now just how many times she was out of line). She taught Lagertha everything she knew, and she was always proud, never shy about bragging to anyone who would listen to her talk about her 'little warrior'.

Yeah, she thought she could get onboard with the idea of a baby. The gods wanted it, Idun had said as much. She couldn't see herself being like Ama and staying home doting over the child all day, but she could be a mom like Brenda.

What about Arve? Could he do it? That mattered less to her than it should. It was simple for her. Either he would be a part of their lives, or she would kill him. She liked him a lot, and was working towards love, but he shouldn't have any illusions.

Still she shouldn't shut him out, she had to let him know how she felt.

She couldn't mention the baby right away, if she did, and Gardi got wind of it, he would ground her. She could give him a little something though. She didn't even have to mean it, she could just say it to gauge his reaction.

"Hey Arve." she said.

"What's up, elsker?" he replied.

"Jeg elsker dig." she said.

"Jeg tager ikke afsted." he said. "I love you too, I thought you knew that."

"I hope that is true, and you *better* not be going anywhere." she said. "I need to tell you something."

"You're pregnant." he said.

"How did you know?!" she asked.

"Don't you remember?" he asked. "I have 5 sisters. I probably knew before you did."

"Let's not tell my father just yet." she said. "I want to fight at least one battle before I get taken out."

"I know better than to argue." he said. "I only ask that you think seriously about it after Lindisfarne. I don't want to get in your way, but you *are* carrying my child."

"Wow." she said. "I'm impressed."

"I'm here in any capacity that you want." he said. "Hopefully, that includes marriage and a family, but you're a little different, Lagertha. You might not want that. We'll go at whatever pace you're comfortable with."

"I could seriously go in that direction." she said. "I just wanted to get your take on it first. You made the right choice. If you didn't want to be involved, I would have to kill you."

"Might be funny if I didn't know you're serious." he said.

Good, then we know where we stand on this." she said. "It would be such a waste to kill you."

He feigned a stab to the heart and a dramatic fall backwards as if he was in the throes of death.

"Don't be a smartass!" she said. "This is serious!"

"I may be a little cocky, sweetheart, but I'm not stupid." he said. "If I wasn't willing to go all the way with you, I never would have started it."

"Hmmm...I thought it was me that started it." she said.

"No, don't you remember?" he said. "It was all part of my diabolic plan. First I let you almost kill me, then I let you nurse me back to health, working you the whole time. I even threw another woman in for good measure. It's Arve's formula for hooking babes. It works every time."

She looked at him puzzled.

He winked at to her let her know it was a joke.

"You're a real comedian, Bjørnsson." she said. "It's too bad that you won't be able to employ Arve's formula any more. You cheat, you die. Remember that."

"I don't know how I could forget." he said. "Besides, I already have the best woman available."

"For you, I'm the *only* woman available." she said. "Not even a meaningless roll in the hay. I'm serious. It got more serious when we made a baby."

"I know, sweetheart." he said. "Jeg tager ikke afsted. I mean it. I'm here for you. But after Lindisfarne, I am going to have to ask you to take it easy. I won't go to Gardi, but this is serious. The legends say that he didn't let your mother fight when she was pregnant. I just want both of you to be safe. I hope you understand."

"That's very sweet." she said. "I'll have to let you know."

14

Alfdis was frazzled. Freki had been out all night and a significant part of the day. He had *never* been gone this long before without checking in.

She knew that there was some stress lately with the crisis with Erika and Magna, but he could have the decency to let her know that he was alive!

He didn't even see it as a crisis! Their immortal souls were in danger, and he didn't care! His was too! How could he not see the truth?

Just then he stumbled in the door.

"Where have you been?!" she cried. "I've been worried sick!"

"I went to a party with Henry." he said.

"For a day and a half?" she asked. "Must have been some party! I thought you were going fishing."

"I told you that because I didn't want you to be upset." he said. "It wasn't your kind of people. You would have hated it."

She sniffed the air suspiciously. Her eyes narrowed and her face tightened.

"Why do you smell like sex?!" she said.

He was tired. Too tired to argue, and too tired for witty retorts. Too tired to make something up, too tired to lie.

"Probably because I had sex with a woman I met at the party." he said. "I think I may have been drugged too. I can't talk about this now. I'm too tired. We'll talk about it when I wake up."

She was dumbstruck as he walked into the bedroom and drew the shade. She wanted to confront him about this, but somehow with a few words he had diffused the situation and was off the hook for the time being.

He knew that he would answer for it later, but he was setting the timetable. They would discuss it when he was ready.

It was strange that she felt powerless to argue. He had never stood up to her in that way. He always let her make the rules. She was so shocked that she just let him go to sleep.

* * *

As they approached the church, Gardi was surprised to find a small welcoming party. He figured that they would all be down in Wessex helping King Alfred.

Maybe he doesn't *need* any help, he thought nervously.

Why was he fucking around with Lindisfarne? He should be down there. We head south after this. What was he thinking? Erik had told him how serious it was, but he *had* to raid first. Now he was wasting valuable time chasing gold.

It wasn't entirely about rewarding the men this time either. He had to admit (at least to himself) that he was pissed at Guðrum. It was so simple a child could have done it, yet he managed to fuck it up. Why should he help? If it was up to him, he may very well have let Guðrum fail miserably.

The thing that made him come was honor. The honor of all of Scandinavia was at stake.

He knew that it was already too late. He didn't know how he knew, he just did. This phenomena had appeared to him recently, yet he didn't know why. Suddenly he knew what was happening in many situations without any logical explanation. And it was never wrong. He was sure that the gods were involved.

He thought back to that day in 824 when everything changed. It still amazed him. He was by no means a spiritual man, yet the gods chose him to carry their message. Now it wasn't unusual at all. Nothing surprised him. If he saw a pig in flight screaming across the sky, he would simply shrug his shoulders and move on to the next thing.

He looked over at Lagertha. A disturbing thought entered his brain. She's pregnant. He knew it was true, and he knew that she knew as well. Her eyes met his and a dazzling smile appeared on her face. He looked directly back at her.

He looked at her and thought what are you doing? Her smile sank into a nervous frown.

He heard her voice in his head.

It clearly said "How does he know?"

I don't know how I know, but you need to go back. I won't have you fighting while you carry my grandson, I didn't allow it for your mother, and I damn sure won't let you, he thought.

She vanished into thin air before everyone's eyes.

* * *

Baldur was shocked to see Lagertha disappear. What happened? She had been looking forward to this for a long time. What was worse, she looked scared before it happened.

It was something he had never seen. His little sis was the toughest woman he knew. He noticed that she seemed fine before his father looked over at her, then she looked scared and vanished. What was going on?

He would find out later, now he had to concentrate on the battle. There was a small group of men defending the religious houses, but not much to worry about.

Once things started getting wet, he figured anyone who was left would run for their lives. His crew alone could probably handle it fairly easily.

He knew the drill. Hack a few up, do some disturbing things with their body parts, and watch the rest of them flee.

It would be easier to arrange a payoff, but it would be more fun this way. The English were perfectly willing to pay the Vikings to go away. It was disgusting. What sort of man would prefer to pay for his safety instead of defending his honor like a man? That was the problem with these English. They were cowards. He looked the group over.

They weren't all Englishmen. He recognized Kalman and Bergelmir from Kattegat. Traitors. He silently swore to himself that they would be the first to go.

* * *

"It really doesn't matter." he said. "It's over. It's been over for quite some time now. I don't need a lawyer, judge, or priest to tell me or give me permission. I'll be by to see Kirsten."

"Like hell you will!" she shrieked. "I won't have you poisoning her mind! I might not be able to save the rest of you, but she still has a chance!"

"Poisoning her mind? With what?" he asked. "I don't believe in anything, remember? Besides, you still have Aesir."

"Who knows *what* he's up to now!" she said. "He's been with the King's army for 5 years now. I can't believe that you're letting the family fall apart like this!"

"Not to worry, Alfred is a good Christian." he said. "I'm sure Aesir's soul is safe. He wouldn't *dare* go against his new master."

"And what about Erika and Magna?" she cried. "I don't want to lose any of you!"

"You're not losing us. Your children love you. *I* love you. We have just grown apart." he said "I need something more. I need to be stimulated intellectually. You need someone to support you spiritually. You have to agree that neither of us is suited to fill those roles for each other."

"I can try." she said meekly.

He looked at her. She was serious, and he knew it. He couldn't understand why she still wanted to continue with this farce of a relationship.

"Why would you want to?" he asked.

"When we made our vows, it was for life, for me." she said. "It doesn't matter what gods we said them to. I am yours, and you are mine. We have created life. A beautiful family. Let's not throw it away."

"What about your church?" he asked.

"I still believe that Jesus Christ is my savior. I want you to believe it too, but not at the cost of our marriage. I will give you time." she said. "In the meantime, I can try to learn about the things you're interested in. I'll back off of the girls, and let them make their own choices. Can you give us a chance?"

He looked at her again. She was scared. She was broken, and appeared to be giving up. He had to admit that he had wanted this for a long time, but was it too late? Could he give it another try? He never stopped loving her, he was just appalled at what she had become.

"I need to go for a walk." he said. "I'll think about it. You don't think it's too late? Maybe we've gone too far?"

"I'll never go far enough that I can't find my way back to you, Freki." she said. "Jeg elsker dig. It's never too late."

She hadn't spoken Danish to him in years. He was actually surprised that she still remembered it. She was really putting it all out there.

"I'll be back soon. I need to clear my head. I'll give it some serious thought." he said.

"Please do." she said. "I want you back."

He walked out the door.

How did he do that? She had always been the strong one. He stood up to her *one time*, and she fell apart. Why? She answered her own question. She didn't want to lose him.

No matter how she felt about the church and religion in general, without Freki, it didn't matter. After all she spent most of her life as a pagan, and all of her adult life with him. She didn't know or even *want* to know about Jesus until she got to England. She was happy in Denmark, happy worshiping the Norse gods. What was it that got her into Jesus in the first place? Audrey.

Audrey had a very strong personality, and she wanted to tell everyone who would listen about Jesus. Alfdis was curious at first, and being a very spiritual being in her own right, she listened, and they became friends.

The thing was, Audrey never wanted to hear about the Norse gods. It didn't bother Alfdis so much, she was learning about Jesus, and some of it was beginning to sink in. She couldn't pinpoint the exact moment, but she had become a full-fledged Christian.

She thought about the Norse gods. There was a time when she was a devout believer in them. How did Audrey convert her so easily? Her father in law was immortal, yet still she turned her back on her first gods. Audrey was convincing, and she never let up.

She was probably ready for something new anyway. Moving here from Denmark, making a new home, she wanted to fit in. Maybe if *everyone* here wasn't so religious it would have been easier to resist. They were the only Danes in the neighborhood.

She wanted to make a good impression, and before long she had started to believe. She faked it at first, she had to. She couldn't go from what she was to what she eventually became overnight.

Now she was looking at both the Norse gods and Jesus in a new light. How could Freki not believe *anything*?

* * *

He walked down the path with his head down. What was he going to do? Could it be the way it was before? Was there even a chance?

A butterfly floated past his head and put itself directly in his path.

"Follow me." it said.

He rolled his eyes. Not this again! Whatever Edward dosed him with would have to have worn off by now, he slept for 9 hours.

He followed the butterfly. Soon they were at a clearing where the woman who said she was his mother was sitting cross-legged.

"And how is your metamorphosis coming along, Freki?" she asked. "Has that hallucinogen worn off yet?"

"It would appear not." he said. "How are you, *Mother*?"

"Quite well." she replied. "She is right, you know. You belong together."

"How could two such different people belong together?" he asked.

"You are not so different." she said. "Right now she is seriously considering returning to the Norse gods."

"And how would you know that?" he asked.

"You forget, son. I am dead. I speak to the gods all the time." she said. "She is still the same girl you married. You will see soon enough."

Was he really talking to this woman? He couldn't imagine Alfdis *ever* leaving her new savior.

"How about we make a little wager?" he asked. "If you're right and she goes back to the Norse gods, I'll go back to her. If you're wrong, you leave me alone forever."

She clucked her tongue and shook her head.

"You shouldn't treat matters of the heart so lightly." she said. "I will do you one better. If I am right, you and I will meet regularly. If I am wrong, I will deliver two horses to your house tomorrow, *and* disappear. Do we have a deal?"

What does it matter? She obviously isn't real, so I won't have to pay either way. When Alfdis doesn't go back to the Norse gods, at least I can call her on it the next time she pops up. Then she'll have to leave me alone.

"As you said, we shouldn't treat matters of the heart so lightly, but I am absolutely sure that I am right." he said. "If you are right, we will meet regularly and I will give Alfdis another chance. That is *if* you are right."

"Then we have a deal." she said. "Your father will be here shortly."

"You keep saying that, but he's not due for months." he said.

"You forget I have inside information, son." she said. "We can make that part of the wager as well if you like. If he doesn't show up within a week, I will gift you 2000 gold pieces. When he does, you must go back to the Norse gods, and you must to talk to him and listen objectively."

"You seem confident." he said.

"My sources are good." she said. "Do you accept my wager?"

He thought about it. What are the odds that I'll have to keep my word to a figment of my imagination? But what if she actually *is* real? She couldn't be. If pop *does* show up, how bad would it be to listen to him a little?

"Okay, but let's stop there." he said. "I never had a problem talking to my dad. If he comes within a week, I promise we'll sit down for a while. I can't make returning to the Norse gods part of the wager. In the unlikely event that you are correct, my heart may not be in it. I can't make that part of the bet."

"I appreciate your honesty. I can accept that you will at least think about going back. The ultimate decision shall be your own. All I ask is that you seriously consider it. But you must listen to your father." she said. "Not just talk but *listen*. He has some valuable information. The gods are watching you, Freki."

He rolled his eyes. *The gods!*

"I promise I'll listen." he said.

"That's all I ask, son." she said. "You must keep an open mind."

With that she slowly faded from view and disappeared before his eyes.

* * *

She was at the camp it was after dark. Stars filled the sky, and she instinctively started picking out constellations.

She wasn't sure what had happened, but her father had sent a clear message that he didn't approve. How did he know?

Where was she? *When* was she? How did she get here?

Suddenly Danu appeared.

"What happened, your highness?" she asked.

"It is common to people who are new to walking. Something back there must have scared you. Those of you that cannot control it yet sometimes experience reflex jumps." she said. "It means that something triggered your fight or flight mechanism and instead of fighting, it sent you on an unplanned walk. What was so scary?"

"My father." she said. "You said back there. Where are we? *When* are we?"

We are 7 days beyond where you were when you took flight." she said. "You're looking at the south end of the North sea. We're near Wessex. How did your father frighten you so?"

"He knows that I'm pregnant." she said. "He sent me a message without speaking. From his mind to mine."

"Telepathy." she said. "Your father has developed a new skill."

"Remember what I have said about interfering with future events." she said. "And Lagertha?"

"Yes your highness?" she asked.

She stopped walking. Danu seemed to be deep in thought for a moment. It looked like she was having a mental struggle over some minor detail. She snapped back to reality and shook her head.

"No. Never mind." she said. "You need to get back to where you were *as soon as possible*. Remember what I said about interfering. You are in a dangerous place, girl."

She took a quick step and pushed hard off the ground taking flight, a phosphorus trail stretching out behind her.

She walked down the beach trying to focus on travelling back in time. She heard some loud voices and giggling from a nearby tent. She recognized the voice as Hildur's, so she went to investigate. There was a strong smell of sex in the air. She walked up to the tent and looked inside. She found Hildur and Arve laying naked together. Not recognizing her, Arve took a swipe at her with his dagger and opened a 2 inch gash on her left cheek.

She remembered what Danu had said about interfering with the future. She clenched her teeth, balled up her fists, and headed off in the other direction.

Her motivation had just jumped considerably. She wanted to go back to a safe time and kill that bastard. Seconds later she was travelling back in time.

* * *

A few minutes later Lagertha reappeared. She was bleeding profusely from her left cheek. Baldur was stunned, but he didn't have time to think about it. Bergelmir was approaching fast.

"Hello, old friend!" he said. "I wish I could say it's good to see you."

"How does it feel to sell out to a false god, traitor?" he replied. "I wonder, will you go to Valhalla or will it be the Jew's heaven? My guess is neither. I think you're going to hell."

"I think you'll find out about the afterlife long before I do." said Bergelmir.

"But that would mean I die before you. That's not going to happen. I'm going to tell you something. Think back to the time you were a Viking." he said. "Tell me if you ever recall me not keeping my word on this. *Your death is on its way.*"

Bergelmir gulped and took a step back. He didn't know why he would have expected anything different. Did he think Baldur would show mercy for old times' sake?

Baldur took a huge horizontal swing and opened an eight inch gash in Bergelmir's belly. His intestines started poking out just a little. Lagertha had killed Kalman and a few other men and was now fighting next to her big brother.

"Let's remind these traitors what it is to be a Viking!" she said.

She started it and everyone joined in.

"Op på de væltede køl

klatre, med et hjerte af stål

kold er ocean's spray

og døden er på vej

med maidens du har haft din måde

hver skal dø en dag!"

(Translation:

Up onto the overturned keel

Clamber, with a heart of steel

Cold is the ocean's spray

And your death is on its way

With maidens you have had your way

Each must die some day!)

Baldur sliced into Bergelmir's neck deeply, which made the weight his head bounce back and forth on a flimsy piece flesh still attached it to his body as he stumbled backwards. There was still just a tiny amount of neck bone keeping it aloft.

Bergelmir was as good as dead, he just didn't consciously know it yet. There was a look of shock frozen on his face, as if to say he couldn't believe that Baldur followed through.

An arrow hit Baldur on the left side of his chest, and he went down. Lagertha looked in the direction it came from, but she couldn't determine the source.

She sliced the rest of the way through Bergelmir's neck, and his head tumbled to the ground. She looked at Baldur.

"Looks like someone got you, sis." he said.

He brought his hand up and lightly stroked the wound on her cheek.

"They must have got me on the way over here." she said.

"Come now, sis. We both know that isn't true." he said. "What really happened?"

"I can't discuss it, Baldur." she said. "Are you okay?"

"Other than the arrow, I'm splendid." he said. "Are you going to make me use the dying man card? What happened?"

"You're not dying." she said.

"That's up for debate." he said. "It sure feels like it. Tell me what's going on, Lagertha."

"Well...do you remember a little conversation we had in the forest a while back?" she asked. "The day I killed the bear?"

"Yeah, I remember." he said.

"Well, it turns out I was right." she said. "I'm getting help from the gods. Let's not worry about that now. Let's get you back to Idonia. She'll patch you up good as new."

The Christians had started to retreat in great numbers, but a few of the former Vikings were still hanging around. There still wasn't a clear path to the monastery or the church.

"Knut! Bjørn! Carry my brother back to the boats! Bring him to Idonia!" she said. "Now! We don't have a second to spare!"

She had been nervous about being a boss, but where her brother was concerned she had no problem getting the crew to respond.

She headed for one of the former Vikings who looked vaguely familiar. She recognized him, it was Leidolf, one of Gunnar's old buddies. She hated to kill a fellow wolf, but under the circumstances she was willing to make an exception. Besides, he was friends with Gunnar, which instantly made him an asshole.

"*LEIDOLF!*" she screamed. "Why are you running away like a pussy? Are you as much of a coward as your buddy Gunnar? If you remember, I took care of him too!"

"Well, if it isn't the little princess!" he said. "I was always disappointed that Gunnar never let me take you for a spin! We can make that happen now if you want..."

He took a swipe at her head, but she ducked easily and plunged her sword into his stomach.

Leidolf was not a good fighter, he always picked weaker opponents. Lagertha was superior fighter, and he knew it.

"How are you going to take me for a spin without a dick?" she asked.

She pulled her sword out and made a swift uppercut between his legs. The sword landed in about the middle of his chest.

"Do you see what I did there?" she asked. "I do it all the time. I over swung. See I wanted to make you suffer, but I got excited. Now you're dead, whether you know it or not. You got me so wound up that it ruined all of my fun. I may as well end it now."

She put her foot on his chest and pried her sword out. She took one more look at him.

"You're pathetic." she said.

She reached her sword back far to her left and swung it hard, decapitating him.

She spat on him.

"You got off easy, Leidolf." she said. "Arve won't be so lucky."

She started scanning the scene for Arve, but she didn't see him.

Suddenly, she started to wonder about something. At this point he hasn't even committed the offense I'm punishing him for. Can I punish him for future crimes? Has he been sleeping with Hildur all this time?

7 days. It's not long enough after I disappeared for him to be with someone else. Unless he was already with her. How was that future possible anyway? Didn't I come back? Is that what would have happened if I didn't? She was confused. Danu was right, making changes in time fucks things up. Just *seeing* the future fucks things up! She couldn't even figure out why he was with Hildur in *that* future. Was it an alternate reality? Hell, maybe there's an alternate reality where I don't even exist!

She looked over the scene, and it appeared that they had a clear path to the church and the monastery. The cowards had fled, and the brave ones were all dead.

She saw Arve lumbering towards the church. She ran ahead of him and blocked his path.

"What's the matter, elsker?" he asked. "Oh, that looks nasty! What happened?"

"Like you don't remember!" she said.

"No, I don't." he said. "Is there something I'm missing here?"

She thought about it. Of course he didn't remember, because it hadn't happened yet! Then where did the cut come from?

She was smart, but the whole space-time thing was messing with her brain. She wished she never acquired this power. Suddenly she knew how her father must feel almost all of the time.

"What about Hildur?" she asked.

"What *about* her?" he said. "We're friends."

"Is that *all*?" she asked.

"You're acting really strange." he said. "Did something happen?"

"No, but something is going to happen." she said. "I meant what I said Arve. You cheat, you die."

"Why would you think that?" he said. "Does this have something to do with your little disappearing trick?"

"What?" she asked.

"Just before the battle started." he said. "You looked at Gardi, then you just disappeared. A few minutes later, you were back."

"Really?" she said. "I bring up your fidelity, or lack thereof, and you come back with *this*?"

"I don't know what you're talking about!" he said. "I haven't done anything!"

She looked him over closely. Damn it! She couldn't tell! That was one of the things that bothered her about him, she could never tell if he was lying.

"Never mind!" she said. "Go get Ari, and Floki, and whoever else you can find. Let's get the treasure back to the ships."

"So tell me, who slashed your face?" he asked.

"You did." she said. "But I don't blame you for not remembering, it hasn't happened yet. It doesn't happen for 7 days."

"What?!" he asked.

"I'll give you one chance…and you should take it." she said. "Stay away from her. If you don't, it ends badly for you."

He gulped, and for a split second he looked guilty, but then it was gone. She couldn't tell if it actually happened. I'm probably paranoid, she thought. *But I did see it with my own eyes!*

"I think maybe you took one to the head, because you're not making sense." he said. "I'll get the guys together and get the loot."

"Just remember what I said." she replied. "I hope you *don't* know what I'm talking about, but if you do…"

"Yeah, okay." he said.

"Floki! Ari! Let's load it up!" he said.

Lagertha glared at him.

"What's wrong with her?" asked Floki.

"You figure it out, you tell me." said Arve, shaking his head.

15

"What would you say if I told you that I'm thinking of going back to the old ways?" she asked.

He couldn't believe it! Was that woman actually right? And what kind of trick was that, disappearing into nothing? He was sure there was a scientific explanation, but he couldn't figure it out yet. He needed to talk to Henry.

"Why would you do that?" he asked. "I thought you were saved by Jesus."

"I started thinking about it." she said. "I was so quick to try to make friends here, I let Audrey talk me into it. She never let me talk about the Norse gods...*my gods*. Before long I started to believe in her god. It's a slippery slope, and I fell all the way to the bottom."

"So you're not a Christian anymore?" he asked.

"I don't know what I believe." she said. "I'm leaning towards *my* gods."

"Why do you need *any* god?" he asked. "Is your life that meaningless without one?"

"I just can't accept that all of this was here before we arrived." she said. "That there was no intelligent design and it all happened by chance. That we procreate without help from a higher power."

"So much of it can be explained scientifically." he said. "I can explain how land was created, and how life is formed in the water. It's fascinating what you learn when these things are explained to you."

"But what about the things you can't explain?" she said.

"Like what?" he asked.

"Your father, for example." she said.

The eternal question. He and his intellectual friends had always written it off as a medical anomaly, but that never really sat right with Freki. If it was a medical anomaly, there should be a medical explanation.

"I don't know." he said quietly. "That is the question that has burned in my mind for my whole life."

"Is it so far-fetched?" she asked. "He rescues Idun, and she rewards him with immortality? It's in her power. Life is one of her specialties. Why couldn't it be true?"

"Because it cannot be explained." he said. "And her so called powers probably don't exist."

"*Probably*. So there is some doubt. Not everything needs to be explained." she said. "Can you explain how you've been talking to your mother?"

"How do you know about *that*?" he asked.

"I went to pray to the gods while you were gone. They told me some of the things that have been happening since I abandoned them." she said. "I was so ashamed. I feel so much better now. You should listen to Astrid."

"I don't know who that woman is, but she is *not* my mother." he said.

"There's one way to find out for sure. Summon her when your father is here." she said "He's coming soon. She wants to continue meeting with you, so you should be able to summon her at your own discretion."

She had definitely changed. She said she would, and by the gods she did. *By the gods!* Now he was doing it! She was every bit as devout to the Norse gods as she was to Jesus earlier that day. He didn't want to admit it, but it was an improvement. If he could only get her to believe in science.

"You really are back, aren't you?" he said.

"I feel like I never left." she said. "And Freki? I'm willing to let this one slide, since I can only imagine what a horrible bitch I've been, but you can't sleep with another woman again, okay?"

"Okay. You know that I'm an atheist, don't you?" he asked.

"I am aware that you are not convinced." she said. "That's all right. I love a good challenge. Jeg elsker dig. Jeg er ikke en Kristen, Jeg tror på den sande guder."

"The true gods?" he asked. "This morning there was only one true god, and it was Jesus."

"What a difference a day makes." she said. "I'll give you all the time you need, Freki. There's no pressure. But you must keep an open mind."

"That's what she said." he mumbled.

"What?" she asked.

"Oh…nothing." he said. "I'll try not to dismiss your ideas without thinking them through. I suddenly feel that I have a lot to think about. I'm glad you're back, Alfdis. Jeg elsker dig."

"I love you too, baby." she said.

* * *

"I think she knows." he said.

"How could she?" she asked. "We've been so careful."

"I don't know. I have the feeling that she's getting help from the gods…like her father." he said. "There's been a lot of weird stuff going on. Did you see that shit yesterday? She literally disappeared for like two minutes!"

"You give her too much credit." she said. "I'm pretty sure your eyes were playing tricks on you."

"I think you're forgetting that I'm not the only one in danger here." he said. "Remember Gersemi? And I didn't even fuck her!"

"You need to relax." she said. "Your guilty conscience is making you paranoid."

Maybe she was right. But Lagertha was pretty specific, she even mentioned Hildur.

How could she know? And what was that shit about it not happening yet? He slashes her face in 7 days? Lagertha wasn't making any sense...or was she making the most sense ever? He *knew* that she was in with the gods! But what did they give her? Hopefully not the ability to detect lies! He chuckled.

Was he being paranoid? He didn't think so. There was just too much there for it to be a coincidence.

"Hey." she said. "Remember me? I thought we were going to make love."

He looked at her. She was so sexy. Not that Lagertha wasn't, it was just nice to have something different. He knew he was playing a dangerous game, but he couldn't help himself. He took a quick look to make sure she wasn't around. Maybe I *am* being paranoid, he thought.

* * *

She looked at her reflection in the water. She brought her hand to her cheek, suddenly realizing they her wound was no longer there. A two inch gash that she couldn't get to stop bleeding had disappeared without a trace!

Does this mean it doesn't happen? She hadn't actually caught him doing anything, yet instinctively she knew that he was up to no good. If he was guilty, why had the wound healed? There wasn't even a scar.

Suddenly Danu appeared.

"Your highness!" she cried. "What are you doing here?"

Her eyes flashed.

"You dare to question me?" she spat out.

She bowed her head.

"Apologies, your highness." she said. "I was just surprised."

"I am not used to my subjects speaking to me this way!" she said. "I must remember that you are...different."

Different? What does that mean? I guess it doesn't matter, I should be happy that she's letting it slide.

"Your highness?" she said. "I'm a little confused."

"I cannot help you with this, child." she said. "I have already interfered too much."

"Why did the wound go away, your highness?" she asked. "Does this mean it never happened? Happens? I don't even know how to word it."

"As I just said, child, I cannot interfere any further." she said. "You were fated to catch Arve in this way. What you saw was in the future."

"So he *did* fuck her? *Will* fuck her?" she said. "Is he fucking her right now...your highness?"

"The future is a funny place. It has yet to happen. We can go there, but there is no guarantee that what we see is real." she said. "It is undecided. Always changing. I will tell you what I tell all of my subjects. Trust your instincts, girl. You have always had good judgement."

"My instincts tell me that he's cheating, your highness." she said. "What should I do?"

Her eyes flashed briefly.

"How many times, and how many ways must I tell you that I cannot help you?" she said. "You are testing my patience, child. You must grow up and deal with this on your own. I cannot be there to hold your hand anymore."

Anymore? When had she *ever* been there to hold her hand? She didn't dare argue. She knew that this conversation was over.

"Yes, your highness." she said.

"You did well in battle today." she said. "That will be the last time until after the child is born. You need not worry about your father...*worry about me.*"

Her eyes flashed again.

She shivered with that unfamiliar feeling. *Fear.* At least it only came out when Danu was around, and anyone in the world would understand if they got one glimpse of those red eyes. *She'll kill me without a second thought.*

"Yes, your highness." she said quietly. "As you say."

"What you do with Arve is entirely up to you. He *is* the father of your child, but that is no reason to yield to him." she said. "All of the information that you need to make your decision will come to you in due time. Do not act out of suspicion. You could be wrong."

"Yes, your highness." she said.

Lagertha turned to look and she was gone. Had she even been here in the first place?

* * *

They were camped on a beach near Wessex. Gardi didn't know what to think. She had disappeared, then reappeared a few minutes later.

He knew that she was pregnant. He didn't know how he knew, but he was certain. It was almost like he scared her with his very thought that she better not be fighting with his grandson in her belly. Then she reappeared again moments later and fought anyway.

The moonlight bathed the beach making everything appear light blue. He saw a hooded figure approaching, he could tell it was a woman. She sat down next to him.

"Long time no see." she said.

He instinctively knew who it was.

"How do I know that?" he said. "For you it could have been as little as a minute."

"As I said before, my darling every moment away from you is an eternity." she said. "I'm sorry I didn't get back to you the following day, but you were a little busy."

"Lagertha is pregnant." he said.

"I know, dear." she said. "The real question is how *you* know."

"It's hard to explain." he said. "I seem to have developed the ability to know things instinctively and never be wrong. Not only that, if I'm not mistaken, I can send a thought to another person simply by thinking it."

"Second sight. Telepathy. It seems that you have had a visit from my mother." she said.

"I think I would remember *that*." he said.

"She doesn't always appear to people when she visits. Particularly given your ties to me and your daughters, she may have wanted to stay in the shadows." said Margaret. "There are always the other gods to consider as well. It's a very delicate balance."

"And what makes you think she visited me at all?" he asked.

"It's obvious. You've been given the gift of second sight...with a twist of telepathy it seems." she said. "She gives this gift freely, and of course most of the time people are unaware that it's her. Astrid never knew, and neither did Helga."

"Nothing surprises me anymore." he said. "I have to ground Lagertha. That's not going to be an easy conversation."

"It's already taken care of, elsker." she said. "Danu has been to see her. She has some other things on her mind at the moment, but Danu made it clear that she is to sit it out until after the child is born."

"When you speak Danish to me it reminds me of Astrid." he said. "What other things?"

"Nothing for you to worry about." she said.

She let the hooded robe fall to the sand, exposing her naked body.

"Swim?" she asked.

She sauntered towards the water knowing that he would follow.

He knew that they would make love as soon as they got out of the water.

* * *

He thought about what she said. Was it so far-fetched? He believed it with all of his heart before. Was he *really* thinking about this? Certainly not seriously. How could he? It was all fairy stories.

He had had long conversations with Henry about this. They had decided that everything that happened was caused by the force of another thing happening. Sometimes these forces were unseen. Like the wind, or sound. The way Henry explained it, there was an explanation for everything, some things simply hadn't been revealed yet. Explanations were always on the way, mankind had only learned a tiny fraction of what there was to know. Could this be true? What was he thinking about, of course it was!

Could he go back to the old ways? He thought about it and decided that he just couldn't. He would feel like a fool and a liar. How could he go back to that fantasy world knowing what he knew now? Henry was right. There was nothing out there.

"What are you thinking about?" she asked.

"I don't know." he said. "Maybe how quickly you changed your tune."

"It wasn't quick." she said. "It's been a lifelong process."

"Have you ever considered that it's not true? Any of it?" he said. "That it's all been made up to keep us in line?"

"Keep us in line?" she said. "How does that work?"

"Imagine there are people above us whose job it is to keep the peace." he said. "You know, the Earls, the Kings. They get us focused on the gods, and we devote so much time and energy to them that we don't have time to make trouble."

"Are you forgetting what Vikings do?" she chuckled. "How can you call *that* not making trouble?"

"That's the beauty of it. Who benefits the most when we raid? It would be counterproductive to ban that kind of mischief. The Earls and the Kings need to be paid!" he said. "It's the same with your Jesus. The clergy keep his followers docile, but they require donations to keep the church going and to solicit absolution for the parishioners. It's all a scam."

"Perhaps you're right." she said. "But I'm not taking any chances."

"Who will your god be next week?" he asked.

"It will be the true gods." she said. "I'll never stray again."

He almost believed her. If only he could talk some sense into her! If he could get her to open her mind to science, he could explain it all…well almost all of it.

He had such a hard time taking her seriously while she believed in those myths. He thought of something.

"Would you be willing to meet one of my friends?" he asked. "To talk about religion and other things?"

"I would love to meet your friends…with the exception of the other woman." she said.

Annabel! What would he do about *that*? He had forgotten all about her.

"I would never do such a thing." he said. "I feel horrible about that. I want you to meet my friend Henry. He's a really smart guy."

"I would be happy to, elsker." she said. "What makes him so smart?"

"He's been studying science for years." he said. "He taught me to read."

"You mean those scribblings on parchment?" she said. "And you think I'm crazy?"

"It's an important skill, a whole new form of communication." he said. "And I can write too. It's so much easier to just read what people are trying to say. There are also books. So many books. It makes learning easier."

"So you don't want to talk to people anymore?" she asked.

"You're missing the point." he said. "Suppose I want to talk to King Alfred. I can't because he's not here. But I can write a message and send it to him. Since he can read too, he will read it and write an answer to me."

"But if you're sending him the message anyway, why not talk to him in person?" she asked.

"There are people called messengers. It is their job to deliver messages. Why do you always think in the simplest terms?" he said. "Of course if I'm going to where he is, I can talk to him in person. But if I have business that keeps me here, I can send him a message."

"Couldn't the messenger just tell him what you have to say?" she asked.

"Of course he could." he said, getting a little impatient. "But suppose what I have to say is personal. I don't want the messenger to know my business. I write Alfred a note, and I seal it with wax so he knows that nobody has tampered with it. Then he sends me a reply with his seal."

She could tell that he was getting exasperated. She didn't want to upset him, especially since he seemed to be opening up.

"Of course, elsker." she said. "I see what you're talking about now. Can you teach me?"

He thought about it. It had been a little tough for him to learn, but once he got going it was easy. He figured that it would be the same for her. She was a smart woman, yet she continued to fall for the religious hoaxes. Still, she was showing an interest. If he could teach her to read, all he would have to do is to give her a book for her to see the truth. Was it possible? Could his wife actually break free of those traps?

"I would be happy to." he said. "We can start tonight."

"I guess that means we have a couple of hours to kill." she said. "Can you think of any ideas for that?"

She started loosening her bodice and smiling at him seductively. She was pretty sure that she still had the goods to keep him interested, even though he had cheated with some whore from the party. She decided that the next time he went to a party to go to, she was going to crash it.

He looked deep into her eyes. She had changed. He didn't know how, but she had changed. A week ago, she probably would have shunned sex because of her Christian morals, but here she was laying it right out to him like an animal in heat. Score one for the Norse gods, he thought.

He leaned in and kissed her passionately as she wrapped her legs around him.

* * *

She was walking down the beach trying to focus on something…something she couldn't quite remember. Was Danu just here?

It seemed that she had to do something very important, but she just couldn't remember. Something to do with time. Yes! She needed to go back in time! But to when? And why?

She heard some giggling in a nearby tent. It sounded like Hildur. She went to investigate.

There was a strong smell of sex in the air. She opened the flap of the tent and looked inside. Her eyes had adjusted to the dark long ago, and she couldn't believe what she saw. It was Arve and Hildur laying naked and cuddling in the tent.

She made straight for Hildur in a blind rage, and as she advanced towards her she felt a sharp pain on the left side of her cheek. Arve had slashed her.

Danu had cast a temporary spell of amnesia on her in the hopes of centering her, since Lagertha couldn't stop thinking about what she had seen in the future. She was almost certain that it was pointless because fate was involved, but she liked the kid in spite of herself, and she wanted to help. That was the reason that the wound disappeared, but at that point the memory part of the spell still hadn't taken hold of Lagertha. She still remembered what had happened in the future.

As soon as Lagertha felt the dagger slice her cheek, the spell was broken and it all came rushing back to her.

She knew that she was in the present, so whatever she did, she wouldn't be messing with time.

She backed out of the tent and reached over her shoulder and withdrew her sword from the scabbard. Arve and Hildur followed, and in a single motion she decapitated Arve, and thrust the sword through Hildur's chest on the backswing.

"I warned you, you bastard." she said. "You cheat, you die. I always keep my word."

She wiped her sword off and returned it to the scabbard.

The tent is in a secluded location, which should help with disposal of the bodies, she thought. They probably picked this spot in the hopes that they don't get caught, she thought bitterly.

There was a forest nearby, so she started up the path to the interior. She started a low whistle, slowly getting louder a little bit at a time. She didn't want to cause a commotion, she had to do this quietly…and quickly.

She heard a rustling off to her left, and caught the familiar scent in the air. A lonely wolf loped up to her easily.

"Hello, big boy." she said. "I have a little project for you…and it involves a delicious dinner. Are you interested?"

The wolf nodded his head slowly.

"Good!" she said. "Now go get the rest of the pack, and meet me by the water. Your name is Aiden?"

The wolf nodded and trotted off in the other direction.

She got back to the beach and slung Arve's body over her shoulder and grabbed a handful of his long blond hair to carry his head.

She walked over to the edge of the forest where a small group of wolves were already forming. She dropped Arve in front of them, and rolled his head to Aiden.

"I need you to get rid of this man, and I'm bringing you a woman as well." she said. "I'm sure I don't need to explain myself. You also need to get rid of the tent. I'll bring that out here for you as well. Eat all that you like, but this has to be our little secret."

The wolves started howling appreciatively.

"On second thought, don't worry about the tent." she said. "Just leave their remains where they can be found easily. If they find the bodies, nobody will think about this too much."

She hadn't thought of how to explain their disappearance. The wolves would do nicely. It would appear that the bastard was off in the woods getting some strange, and the next thing he knew they were getting eaten alive. The justice of nature.

If anyone actually figured it out, it was justified, and *anybody* would know it. I have more friends in camp than either of those two, however, it will probably be a while before I have another boyfriend, she thought.

Suddenly she thought of the baby. *She was going to have a baby!* And she just killed its father! Good riddance, she thought. He was no good anyway.

He should have known better! She couldn't believe after all that had happened, after all the warnings, after how things ended with Gunnar, he was still stupid enough to try. What was he thinking?

She got back to the tent and lifted Hildur over her shoulder. And this dumb bitch should have known better too! How could they have possibly thought that this would *ever* end well for them? I'm surrounded by idiots!

She got back to the clearing and dumped Hildur in front of them.

They were already making short work of Arve, they had stripped his arms and legs to the bone and they were gnawing on his torso. Aiden was trying his best to wrap his jaw all the way around his head, but he couldn't quite get it. She took a stone and cracked his head. It held together with a thin strip of skin and bone, but Aiden snapped it in half instantly.

"There." she said. "That should make it easier. Just leave at least a little evidence of what happened here. You don't have to leave a lot, just some bones. The girl is a little small, I'm sorry, but this bastard should be pretty filling."

16

Asgard

"What happened?" asked Odin. "I thought she was under control!"

"You *dare* to ask me *junior*?" she said. "Must I *really* explain this to you? That dumb ass cheated, and these are the results. I tried to fix it, but I can only do so much when fate is involved."

"He served his purpose anyway." said Loki. "I fail to see the problem. If he had such inklings, his days were numbered anyway."

"The problem is that now the child will grow up without a father." said Thor. "I know that a strong masculine influence is pretty low on your list, but it is crucial to normal people. Not everyone is comfortable being as effeminate as you."

"Once again brother, you are confusing intelligence with weakness." he said. "Are you forgetting about the child's grandfather? What better role model could you hope for?"

"Cease this bickering!" said Danu.

Her eyes flashed red, silencing the entire room.

"Loki is right." she said. "Arve has served his purpose. Lagertha is with child. This is what we had hoped for. We must wait at least 9 months before we need to worry about another man for her."

"Good luck making *that* happen!" said Freyja. "By now, every decent man in Scandinavia knows what happens if you cross her! She could use some lessons in grace."

"People have short memories." said Danu. "I know that many of the men are cowards these days, but I must believe that there are still some that are up for the challenge. And those are the ones we want."

"Yes." said Thor, smiling. "I had not thought of that. The stock must remain strong. We cannot have candidates like my brother polluting the bloodline."

"Someone like your brother would be perfect." said Odin. "As long as he also has your qualities. That would be optimal."

"Your father is right." said Idun. "And we must not worry too much about Arve. I have confidence that Gardi will be up to the challenge. Arve would only have been a detriment."

"I must agree with the lifegiver." said Danu. "And I had better not hear you questioning me again, son. You are trying my patience. Does anyone have anything else?"

Nobody dared speak.

Odin jumped in before Danu had a chance.

"Dismissed." he said.

She glared at him but said nothing.

* * *

They paused and started howling in tribute to Lagertha. They really appreciated this little diversion.

"I have to go now, boys and girls, but I'll stop and say hi the next time I'm around." she said.

Several of them came up and nuzzled her and licked her hand.

"Until next time." she said.

She walked back to the beach and headed for the camp.

She wondered how Baldur was doing. She had told him that he would be fine, but neither of them really believed it. It was just something you say.

Idonia really *was* the best, she was almost as good as Vali. She had stabilized him shortly after they got him back, and he was doing as well as he could be. Still, he was in grave condition. Nobody had any illusions that there was much hope. Most men with his wounds would have been dead already, but her brother was tough. He had Brenda's blood running through his veins, as well as Gardi's. If anyone could pull through this, it would be him.

As she approached the camp she met Gardi…and *her* halfway. It was Margaret, Disa's 'mother'.

"Where have you been?" he asked.

"You don't know?" she said. "You seem to be in on everything these days."

"Apparently I had a visit from a friend of yours...and hers." he said. "Lagertha, this is Margaret."

"Yes, the woman who's younger than me, yet she has a daughter who is in her 50s." she said. "Are you saying that Danu visited you? Why would she do that?"

"She gave me a gift." he said. "Second sight and tele...what was it?"

"Telepathy." said Margaret. "Nice to meet you. Where were you?"

"That's probably not the tone to be taking with me." she said.

She glared at Margaret. Who was this woman to speak to her like that? Who did she think she was?

"Answer the question." said Gardi.

"Who is this slut to order me around?" she asked. "Where does she get her nerve?"

"Besvar spørgsmålet. She speaks for me." he said.

"Why does she speak for you? You're standing right here!" she cried.

"Perhaps I put that wrong." he said. "You will give her the same respect that you give me. Why would you call her a slut? You don't even know her."

"She slept with you while you were married to mama!" she said. "And had a baby! Who is my seer, as well as my half-sister! Why are you still involved with her?"

"It is not your place to question me, young lady." he said. "I am your father. Margaret is more important than you know. Besvar spørgsmålet. Where have you been?"

She couldn't believe it! He was taking *her* side. Where did this bitch come from? She is obviously important to daddy, so I better play along. What should I tell them?

"I was off for a walk." she said.

"How's Arve?" asked Margaret.

How could she know about *that*? How does she even know about *him*? She decided to try to play it cool.

"I haven't seen him." she said.

Suddenly a single thought overpowered her mind. *TELL THE TRUTH!*

Gardi was looking directly into her eyes, and she knew that it had to be him. How did he do that?

"Stop it, daddy!" she said. "It seems that you both know the truth already, why are you asking me?"

"It's important to take responsibility for your actions." he said. "Now what happened?"

"I caught him with another woman." she said. "I snapped. They're both dead."

"We need to head back." he said. "We're going up the river inland at dawn."

"What's the rush?" she asked.

"We need to get to the interior as soon as we can." he said. "It's probably too late, but we need to help Guðrum if we can."

"How is Baldur?" she asked.

"He got some help from an unexpected source." he said. "He's going to be fine."

"What source?" she asked.

"An old friend." he said.

He absently watched a falling star plummet to the earth.

"What do we say about Arve?" she asked.

"Don't worry, sweetheart, it won't go any further than us." she said. "Arve has served his purpose."

"Don't call me sweetheart!" she said. "Where does she get the nerve, daddy?"

"Margaret is an old soul." he said. "She takes a familiar tone with everyone, she always has. It's just her way. You need to find a way to get along with her. You two go ahead. I'll catch up with you."

"But why, daddy?" she asked. "Why do I need to get along with *her*?"

"Because she's going to be with us a long time." he said.

* * *

The wolves were busy gnawing on what he could only assume were the remains of Arve and his unfortunate ladyfriend. It was strange that they didn't even acknowledge him as he walked past, but he instinctively knew that they would do him no harm. They were friends with his daughter.

He got to the clearing and waited. He started looking to the heavens to find the constellations.

He found Níðhöggr, the dragon who gnaws at the root of Yggdrasil, the world tree. He saw the Eagle, and Ratatoskr, the squirrel that delivers messages up and down Yggdrasil between the Eagle and Níðhöggr. Further to the east was Durathror, the giant buck, and just south of that was Thjazi's Eyes.

What was taking her so long? Had he misread the sign?

"Why are you so impatient, sweet Gardi?" she said.

"I was not sure I interpreted the sign correctly." he said. "I am glad to see you."

"How are things?" she asked.

"Well...Guðrum is about to lose us all of our gains in England, and there is nothing I can do about it. My son almost died, but thanks to Margaret, he will be fine." he said. "I just had a pretty tense moment with her and my daughter. Oh, and she just killed her the father of her child, but other than that, I am fine."

"The gods never give us anything that we cannot handle, dear. It sounds like things are a little unsettled right now, but that is exactly the situation you are walking into in England." she said. "You will not be successful here, but you already knew that. You are here to set an example. Never forget that people look to you for direction."

"What about Lagertha and Margaret?" he asked.

"Your daughter will have to work up to that. You must remember that she has Brenda's blood running through her veins." she said. "It is rumored that memories can be passed on genetically. We know very little about genetics. I don't need to remind you how Brenda felt about Margaret. You must give it time."

"Yes, of course you are right." he said. "We both know how headstrong she is."

"How headstrong who is?" she asked.

It was Lagertha. She had followed him with a little help from her canine friends.

"Who do you think?" he asked.

"Daddy, I do not know if I can do it." she said. "How can you ask me to tolerate her?"

"You must see the big picture, dear. It is all connected. Margaret is a big piece of the puzzle." she said. "You will see. Right now the most important thing is the child."

"Yes, your highness." she said.

"Such formalities are not necessary with me, sweet child." she said. "Save that for the one with the burning eyes."

"Not so fast." said Gardi. "I do not think that I have ever heard her be so respectful to *anyone* in my entire life!"

"It is a matter of survival with 'the one with the burning eyes'." she said.

Idun smiled broadly.

"Do you not see, sweet Gardi?" she asked. "Your daughter is extremely intelligent. But no more fighting, dear. The gods insist."

"Do not worry about that." she said. "I have already been warned by...well, 'the one with the burning eyes'. Do you know *anyone* who would dare to defy her?"

"Not even Thor." she said. "They are all petrified of her, even Odin. I do not know if you are aware, but he is her son."

"Well, I knew she was old." she said. "Do not worry, I tread *very* lightly with her."

"That is wise." she said. "Are you ready for the challenges in England?"

"As much as I can be in my condition." she said. "Why could I not have gotten pregnant *after* the fighting?"

"It is all as it is supposed to be, elsker. If you had waited, who is to say that you would have found a willing man?" she said. "No, it all happened as it was supposed to. It was fated. It was decided th…"

"Thousands of years ago, we know." finished Gardi.

"The two of you must get back." she said. "You have a long day tomorrow."

"We will be okay." said Gardi.

"And Lagertha?" she said.

"Yes, your high…oh, sorry." she said.

"It is quite all right, my dear." she said. "Try to get along with Margaret. You are not so different. It would please Danu greatly if you try."

"Say no more." she said. "The last thing I want to do is piss her off. It would be a miracle if there was anything I could do to actually *please* her."

"Be careful what you wish for, child." she said. "We live in an age of miracles. Your father is living proof, as are you."

"I am nothing special." she said.

"I must disagree." she said. "Do you know anyone else who can travel through time? Anyone else that has been granted eternal youth?"

"My father." she said.

"Your dear father cannot travel through time, Lagertha." she said. "Very few have that power."

"His new girlfriend does." she said, pouting.

"Margaret is…different." she said. "She came into his life for a reason. We need her. She is not his girlfriend, it is…complicated. Do you have any idea what she has done for you?"

"Other than be rude and arrogant, no." she said. "Oh, right, she slept with my father while he was married to my mother."

"Baldur lives." she said.

Idun paused for a moment to let it sink in. Lagertha looked genuinely confused.

"I had hoped that he would hang on for a while." she said. "I must get back to camp before he goes."

"No, sweetheart, you do not understand." she said. "He lives. As he did before. Margaret gave him life."

"How did that happen?" she asked.

"As I said, child, we live in an age of miracles. Enjoy it while it lasts. There will come a time when the people no longer believe in magic." she said. "Those days will indeed be difficult. Have gratitude for today. Have gratitude for every *moment*. Nothing lasts."

"I cannot make any promises about Margaret." she said. "If she did save my brother, I will give her some credit for that."

"Do you have reason to doubt me?" she asked, raising an eyebrow.

Lagertha looked at her. She hoped she did not offend Idun. She half expected to see her eyes light up.

"I am truly sorry, Idun." she said. "Of course I believe you. It just seems so out of character for *her*."

"And what do you know of her character?" she asked.

Lagertha suddenly wished she could crawl under a rock and hide. Idun was supposed to be the cool one.

"You are right." she said. "I will give her a chance and learn about her character. I am sorry. I am a little emotional."

"That comes with the pregnancy." she said. "Just ask your father. He has had plenty of experience over the years."

She looked at Gardi, who was nodding knowingly.

"We might have to lock this one up." he said.

"Surely that will not be necessary." she said. "Lagertha, if you are feeling particularly stressed, take a little trip. It costs nothing, and I am sure that Danu would agree that you need the practice."

"Of course you are right." she said. "And I will make an effort with Margaret."

"That is all that we ask." said Idun. "It is important. Do not judge her based on the past. If you knew your mothers part, you may not feel the same way."

"I am well aware of my mama's shortcomings." she said. "But still she was my mother. It may be a while before I can warm up to her."

"That is understood." she said. "We did not expect you to be as sisters from the start. Just keep an open mind."

"I promise that I will." she said.

"You two must go back now." she said. "If you have trouble finding gratitude in the little things, at least have gratitude that Baldur has recovered."

She was looking directly at Lagertha. She had had this conversation with Gardi several times already, and expected to have it again in the future...with both of them.

"Thank you for your help, your hig...ahem, sorry." she said. "I will try."

"Thank you, dear." she said.

"And Gardi?" she asked.

"Yes?" he said.

"Do you remember the conversation we had long ago about the possibility that someday you might need to go into hiding, or at the very least keep a low profile?" she asked.

He remembered. She had said that someday people would stop looking at him as blessed, and start looking at him as a heretic. She said there would come a day when people would become scared of what he had become, and he would have to hide.

"I remember." he said.

"That time may be coming soon." she said. "Be prepared, and prepare your family."

"Is it that bad?" he asked.

"There are big changes that are about to happen in England." she said. "Be ready."

It never stops, he thought.

"Okay, we will be ready." he said.

"Have a safe trip the rest of the way." she said.

She pushed off a small rock and screamed across the sky.

"Do you know how long it was before she let me see that?" he asked.

"What, flying across the sky?" she asked. "Danu does it all the time."

H shook his head. He was getting used to her now, but in the beginning, Idun played it pretty tight. He never saw her coming or going, and he never knew when to expect her. She was right. As she kept telling both of them, it had become a different world.

They started back to camp.

"So what does she mean to you, daddy?" she asked. "What about Ama and Brun? What will they think?

"If she's still around by the time we get back, I'll sit down with them." he said.

"You're the one who should be grateful, daddy!" she said. "You get away with *everything*!"

"Even a beggar on the street has something to be grateful for. Everything depends upon your perspective. The beggar doesn't have to handle and provide for hundreds of men and women. His life is simple. Ours is not. Our rewards are greater, yet so is our effort." he said. "I have had that conversation with her on many occasions. Listening to her tell it to you helped to emphasize the point. Gratitude is everything. It truly does create prosperity and happiness. If I am grateful for what I have, more comes to me. If I dwell on what I don't have, more things disappear. It truly is that simple. I don't know why it is, it just is."

She looked at him in amazement. He really believed this. Could it be true? Is that all it takes? What did she have to lose? Nothing. What did she have to gain? Everything. She decided that she would try it.

"Thank you, daddy." she said. "I heard what she was saying, but I was just being polite. To hear you talk this way makes me want to try."

"It costs nothing, and you have everything to gain." he said.

My exact words, she thought.

"I know that you have this new skill, daddy, but please stay out of my head." she said. "Trust me, you may find things up there that you won't like."

"I wasn't actually up there this time. And if you think you can shock me, think again. I've seen almost everything in my life before I ever had this gift." he said. "Believe me when I tell you that I don't need to cheat to know what you're thinking. Your face and eyes reveal everything."

"*Really*?" she said. "And what am I thinking now?"

"You're thinking about what you would do to Margaret if she didn't have protection." he said.

"Get out of my head." she half joked.

17

"You know what this means, don't you?" she asked.

"Is their way of doing things so bad?" he asked. "They live an educated life. They don't live by fairy stories. Although many of them believe in Jesus Christ, many also take science into account. They don't live like cavemen as we did in Scandinavia. I just want you to try to understand the logic of it."

"So now our people are cavemen?" she asked. "I just want you to keep an open mind. We have lost our hold in England thanks to that idiot. I want to go back to Denmark."

There she goes with the same words that Astrid said. *Keep an open mind.* Astrid! Now *he* was doing it! Did he actually believe that this figment was his mother?

"I don't know if I can go back there." he said. "There are no books, no smart people. I want to continue to learn."

"What better way to learn than to teach?" she said. "You teach me, and we can teach them together. I want you to be happy. We can bring books with us. We can teach the cavemen to read."

Suddenly a dog approached them. To Alfdis, it sounded like he was just barking, but to Freki it was a conversation.

"Go to the river." said the dog. "Your father will be here shortly."

"He's not due for months." said Freki.

"He'll be here within the hour." he said. "You must tell him about Guðrum. He probably already knows, but you should meet him. You made a promise…"

"Yeah, right. I forgot." he said. "How do you know about that?"

"Who do you think sent me?" he asked.

"Right. I'm still not sure I believe all that." he said. "But here I am talking to a dog, so why not? I'll head down there."

"I'll let her know." said the dog.

"Okay, thanks." he said.

He shook his head. Did that just happen?

Alfdis was standing there with her mouth open and a blank stare in her eyes. She managed to gain her composure enough to speak.

"Did you just talk to that dog?!" she asked.

"Apparently." he said.

"And you have the nerve to tell me that you don't believe in the gods?" she said.

"I'm sure there is an explanation." he said, doubtfully. "Maybe there is something in the water that is making us both hallucinate."

"What did he say?" she asked.

"He said to go down to the river because my father will be here shortly." he said. "We need to tell him about Guðrum."

She shook her head. Unbelievable! Why him? He doesn't believe in *anything*!

Suddenly she went into a blank stare for about 30 seconds.

"Um, honey?" she said. "I think I just got a message from your father. He wants us to meet him at the river. Did you get any message?"

"No, I didn't hear anything…except from the dog." he said. "I guess we better head down there."

"So the dog tells you, and I get confirmation from your father." she said. "How could you understand that dog and not your own father?"

"I don't know." he said.

She smacked her forehead.

"I know what it is!" she said. "You couldn't understand your father because you don't believe in the gods anymore!"

"That's ridiculous!" he said. "Then how do you explain the dog?"

He realized his mistake immediately.

"That's simple." she said. "You talking to the dog is proof that the gods exist. They're jumping up and down trying to get your attention. Will you listen?"

"It appears that I have no choice at the moment." he said. "Come on, let's get down to the river."

As they walked towards the river, Freki started getting an eerie feeling. It wasn't anything that he could put his finger on, it was like...déjà vu. Like he had done all of this before. As he passed trees, he remembered them from this mysterious time in the past that he had made this trip before.

Probably the last time I went fishing, he thought.

"You just can't do it, can you?" she asked. "Suspend your disbelief. Believe that there is something out there greater than yourself."

"Can you prove that?" he asked.

"No, and that's the beauty of it." she said. "Even though I can't prove it, I see evidence of it every day. You would too if you recognized the magic that is all around us."

"Magic gave up on me long ago." he said.

"No, elsker, you gave up on magic." she said. "It has always been here, waiting for you to come back...waiting for *me* to come back."

She was truly the girl he met in Denmark so long ago. Could he ever be the same man? Knowing what he knew now?

He didn't exactly believe in magic, but some really strange things had been happening lately. He hadn't ruled out his theory of something in the water, but it seemed to be getting less and less likely. Could it be?

NO! He was not thinking this! He needed to talk to Henry, or Annabel- Hell, I would even take Edward at this point, just for a little sanity!

As they rounded the bend his jaw dropped. The unmistakable dragonhead on the front of his father's boat was gliding through the water, heading straight for them. On the shore in a small clearing sat the woman who claimed to be his mother. She was smiling widely, beckoning him to come over.

"Who is that?" asked Alfdis.

"My mother?" he said. "I don't know. I guess we're about to find out."

They walked over and sat down.

"Hello." she said. "I guess this must be Alfdis. I was hoping we would meet."

"You must be Astrid." she said. "Freki still isn't convinced, but I'm working on him."

"All will come in time, child." she said.

She smiled, and glitter seemed to surround her face, making it look like a shiny snow shower had just fallen only in her vicinity.

Freki couldn't stop staring at the boat. He couldn't believe that this was actually happening. It was just like she said. His father had come over to help Guðrum, but it was too late. Could it all be true?

His father came out from behind the wheel and waved at them. On the boat behind them was Lagertha. He couldn't believe how much she had changed since the last time he'd seen her. She was still the awkwardly tall girl he remembered from the last time, but there was something different. She seemed more confident. Gardi beckoned to Astrid.

"I heard you were going to be here." he said. "I see you've met your son."

"He doesn't believe that I'm his mother." she said.

"Is that true, Freki?" he said. "She came all this way, and you don't acknowledge her?"

He felt like he was falling, flying through the air towards the ground at a great velocity. He looked up, and he saw his father as he passed by.

"Come and find me, Freki." he said. "We need to talk."

Suddenly he woke with a jolt.

It was just a dream, he thought. Then he remembered what his father had always told him about his mother. Her belief that there is no such thing as 'just a dream'.

Was this happening?

He turned to Alfdis and sighed.

"We need to get down to the river." he said.

* * *

"We might still be in time." said Baldur.

"No, there's no doubt about it. It's too late. We still have to go, but I'm warning you in advance that we won't be successful." he said. "We must not let on to the crew. They're looking to us for guidance. How would it look if we just gave up?"

"But I'm not giving up." he said.

"Neither am I." said Gardi. "I'm just being realistic."

"But how do you know?" he asked.

"I was recently visited by an ancient goddess who gave me the gift of second sight." he said. "It's stronger than my second wife, Astrid, Freki's mother. I don't know why she gave me this gift. Perhaps so I know about these things in advance."

"I hope you're wrong, pop." he said.

"So do I, but I know I'm not." he said. "That idiot trapped himself, and now we're going to pay the price."

"Okay, if you know so much what's going to happen?" he asked. "What price will we pay?"

"Go get your sister, I'll tell you everything." he said. "She should know this too."

"Okay, I'll be right back, pop." he said.

"Do you really think it's best to tell them everything?" asked Margaret.

"I don't see why not." he said. "They will know soon enough anyway."

"Are you sure you're not just showing off your powers?" she asked.

"Have you ever known me as a man that craves attention?" he asked. "They're my children. I want them to be prepared. After this is over, we may very well need to go into hiding."

"Okay, I guess it makes sense when you put it that way." she said.

"Maybe you should go down below." he said. "I think Lagertha's trying, but she's not quite there yet. It's for your own safety."

"You don't need to make excuses to talk with your kids in private." she said.

"Trust me, I'm not." he said. "She's twice as bad as Brenda. Now go."

"You don't need to tell me twice." she said.

She was just walking away as Baldur and Lagertha got there.

"I still don't like her, daddy." she said.

"Speaking for myself, I like her a lot." said Baldur.

"That's just because she saved your life!" she said.

"Gratitude, sweetheart." said Gardi. "Remember what's important. Her saving your brother's life is a good reason to be grateful. It's also a good reason to give her a chance."

"I guess you're right, daddy." she said.

He silently wondered if there was any truth to what Idun was saying about genetics. Was it possible that Lagertha had a genetic proclivity to hate Margaret that wasn't her fault? Passed down by her mother? I guess anything is possible, he thought.

The rest of the crew were sleeping. They were heading up the river Thames, moving inland towards the battle. The sun would be coming up soon.

"Sit back, this might take a while. You both know how I know this, perhaps Lagertha understands better." he said.

"And why would that be?" asked Baldur.

"She's more familiar with Danu- the goddess who helped me." he said.

"It's true." she said. "Daddy's right. She is very powerful. Idun herself said that she gave him the gift."

"You talked to Idun?" he said, bewildered.

"Not as often as daddy, but every now and then." she said. "Remember? I told you what happened?"

"Yeah, I guess." he said. "I didn't really take you seriously."

"It's true." said Gardi. "She has some powers that I don't even have. Let me tell you what's going to happen."

They both looked at him eagerly.

"It is quite well possible that Guðrum has already surrendered to Alfred. Alfred has had him under siege for the last two weeks, and has cut off any supplies to him. Essentially he's starving him out. Guðrum will negotiate a peace that will become known as the 'Treaty of Wedmore'. He will give Alfred hostages, and pledge an oath to cease molesting his Kingdom. He will settle for a fraction of our gains to the north of Wessex called East Anglia. These lands will eventually become known as Danelaw, a refuge for Scandinavians in England. None of these things are the worst of it. Guðrum will also convert to Christianity. He will accept Alfred as his adoptive father. His Christian name will be Æthelstan. The conversion to Christianity will be a double edged sword. Not only will we suffer the shame of surrender, but politically he will be beholden to Alfred for the rest of his life as a Christian. His oath to the treaty will become legally binding as a Christian, and of course, Alfred will legally be his father." he said.

"Is there nothing we can do to stop it?" asked Baldur.

"It is fate." said Gardi. "Even if we stopped it, something equally bad or worse would happen. That is the nature of fate. In any case, it is my opinion that this has already come to pass."

"That's a lot to take in." said Lagertha. "Has he no pride?"

"He put himself in a difficult position." said Gardi. "He got overconfident. He nearly took Wessex. Then Alfred turned the tables on him. It was conform or starve. I hate to give him an excuse, but he had no choice."

"He had a choice." said Baldur. "He could have fought like a man."

"He should have done that earlier." he said. "By the time he realized it, it was too late. I'm not giving him a pass. I'm incredibly pissed. There's just nothing we can do. We need to continue as though we don't know any of this. Keep the crew positive. Our job is to set an example. A better example than 'King' Æthelstan."

"That name! I guess it suits him." said Lagertha. "A fucking Christian name!"

"It was the name of Alfred's eldest brother." he said. "And don't even think about him going back on his word. This is fated. There's nothing we can do. Do you remember what she said before she left, Lagertha?"

"About going into hiding?" she asked.

"Yes." he said. "We need to be ready. When news about this gets back to Scandinavia, a lot of people will think about Christianity. We may need to disappear."

"Disappear?" asked Baldur.

"Move on. To somewhere that nobody knows about us." he said. "Hell, maybe there will be others that feel the same way. We could start a new colony. I've heard that there are more lands to the north and the west."

"We'll do whatever we have to do." he said.

"We need to find your brother." he said.

"Leif, Kol and Bjørn are all here." he said.

Sveyn had died in battle 12 years ago.

"Your older brother." he said.

"Freki." he said.

He had thought quite a bit about Freki over the last couple of months. Perhaps it was old age setting in, but he wanted his brother to know that he still loved him. He had always admired him.

When he was younger, he never understood why he didn't like to fight. Now that he was older and had seen a lot more of the world, he realized that Freki had other talents.

He could plan a battle better than anyone he knew including his father. Maybe Guðrum should have found *him*, he thought.

"I would really like that." he said.

"Me too." said Gardi. "I worry about him. His wife has too much influence on him."

"Don't worry about it, daddy." she said. "Remember what Disa said?"

"And who is Disa?" asked Baldur.

"It's a long story." he said. "Let's just say she's a seer in Kattegat that your sister and I have both been seeing."

He held up his hands.

"Don't mind me!" he said. "Maybe someday I'll get an invitation to your secret little club!"

"It's not like that." said Lagertha. "Neither of us asked for this."

"You could take a lesson in gratitude as well, young man." he said. "Be grateful you don't have the responsibility."

"It's a little weird you calling me 'young man' when I'm 26 years older than you." he said.

"You're really not, you just look it." he said.

"Thanks. I feel much better now." he said.

"Your brother..." he said. "He doesn't believe in anything now."

"What about Alfdis?" she asked.

"I don't know." he said. "For some reason I have hope for her now. I think she has come back to our gods."

"Are you kidding, daddy?" she said. "Don't you remember how she was the last time?"

"That was 10 months ago." he said. "What was going on with you 10 months ago? Would you say there have been a lot of changes?"

"That's different." she said.

"How so?" he asked. "Do you think you're the only one the gods care about? Have you given up on your sister in law?"

"No, it's just that she was so devoted to Jesus!" she said. "It made me sick! Freki is too smart for that."

"Yet he has nothing now." he said. "He has no god."

"Believe me, that's better than being like his wife!" said Baldur.

"Like I said, I have a good feeling about her." he said. "We might just hope she has enough influence on him to get him to change his mind again."

"Are we talking about the same woman?" she asked. "Because that would truly be a miracle."

"Hmm. It seems to me that someone said recently that we are living in an age of miracles." he said.

"Using *her* words against me." she said.

"I'm not the one who brought it up." he said.

"I don't care what you think, I don't like that woman." she said.

"And what did you think of her when we were all still in Denmark?" he asked.

"That's different, and you know it, daddy!" she said. "She still believed in the true gods then! Now she's been brainwashed by her new neighbors and she's a Christian!"

"What would you say if she actually did go back to the Norse gods?" he asked.

"I would have to *see* that to believe it!" she said.

"Well, you're about to get your chance." he said.

As they rounded the bend in the river, they saw Freki and Alfdis standing by the shore. Gardi's was stunned when he saw them. He knew that Freki and Alfdis would be there, but he was not expecting what he saw next. It was Astrid.

18

"Make shore, and pull it up!" shouted Gardi.

Many of the Vikings were still a little groggy, it was just after sunrise, and they had just woken up. They manned the oars and steered the boat in to shore, got out and heaved it up by the mooring lines. Most of them that had been around long enough to remember him were surprised to see Freki. The crew had always liked him, even though he wasn't as bold of a warrior as his brother.

Gardi was still assessing the scene. He had seen a lot of strange things since the gods blessed him. He never expected to see Astrid again. Was she real? He was about to find out.

"Did you know about this?" he asked.

"How could I?" said Margaret. "I can only assume that this is Astrid. It's as much of a surprise to me as it is to you."

"Wow. And I thought you knew everything." he said.

"I'm not the one with the second sight." she said. "You didn't pick up on it?"

"I didn't see a thing." he said. "How did you know it was her?"

"An educated guess." she said. "She's with your son...*her* son. She is just as I imagined she would look."

"I think the two of you would have gotten along great." he said. "You have a lot in common."

"More in common than either one of us had with Brenda, I would guess." she said.

"Sure. But that's not a small club." he said. "I've known a few rough women, but not many who could compete with her."

"There's one that comes to mind." she said.

"She's her mother's daughter." he said. "There is so much of her in Lagertha that it's hard to tell the difference sometimes."

"There's a lot of you in there too." she said.

"See, that's what I'm talking about." he said. "As horrible as she's been to you, you still find the good."

"Anything that is a part of you is special." she said. "The gods wanted her. Did you know that? They waited patiently, and I can't say they weren't a little nervous after 5 boys."

"But it was fated...thousands of years ago." he said.

"Don't be a smart ass." she said.

They disembarked and Gardi went up and gave his son a long hug.

"Do you recognize this woman?" asked Freki.

"It's your mother." he said.

"I just lost a huge bet, dad." he said.

He hadn't actually promised to go back to the Norse gods. But he did tell her that he would *seriously* consider it. Freki was not a man who took wagers lightly. He felt an obligation to her to give it as much of a chance as he possibly could. Could he do it? He had to admit that there was some pretty wacky stuff going on, and one explanation would be the gods.

He had lost every part of the bet. He was on the hook to give Alfdis another chance, meet with his *mother* regularly, and seriously consider going back to a religion that didn't make any sense to him.

His *mother*! It was bizarre just to think it, let alone speak it. The only 'mother' he ever knew was Brenda, and she gave him very little attention. She kept up appearances for Gardi's sake, but he knew that she only cared about her own children.

Who was that woman who was with him? She looked vaguely familiar.

He saw his brother Baldur getting off the boat. He thought about their childhood. When they were little, they were great friends and they played together every day. There was a woman, one of the servants who always encouraged them to play together and be friends. It was his earliest memory. He was no more than a few years old.

Suddenly it all came back to him in a rush. It couldn't be! She would have to be in her 70s or 80s by now! But there was no mistaking it. It was her. As she followed his father back towards his mother He shook his head in disbelief. He actually tapped himself on the side of the head as if to knock something back into place.

"Margaret?" he asked.

She turned around and smiled.

"Freki, my little sweetheart!" she said. "You remember me!"

Baldur was watching the exchange, and it seemed to dawn on him at the same time. He ran up to them.

"See, I knew that I knew you!" he said. "I've been trying to figure it out ever since you showed up. You're Margaret, our servant from when we were little! Why are you so young? Are you immortal too?"

"No, dear." she said. "Let's just say that the gods have given me a different gift. It is the same gift that your sister has been given."

"She still hasn't told me the whole story on that." he said.

"Wait a minute! The *gods* have helped my sister as well?" said Freki.

"I understand that you have been having a little trouble lately understanding the gods Freki." she said.

"I have." he admitted. "But it seems that I must seriously consider them again now. A very unlikely eventuality has come to pass, and now I have to pay up on what turned out to be a foolish wager."

"But was it so foolish, dear?" she said. "The end result will change your life."

"How do you know about it?" he asked.

"I have good sources." she said.

The same thing *that woman* said, he thought. *My mother! I have a mother! It was true after all! But how is she here? Isn't she supposed to be dead?*

* * *

Gardi walked up to her. He couldn't believe it. It really was her.

"Is it really you?" he asked.

"Yes, elsker." she said. "But only for a while."

"What do you mean?" he asked. "Why are you so young? And how are you here? And why can't you stay?"

"I am as I was when I died. The 24 year old beauty who was your second wife. I came back because our son was in trouble." she said. "I guess it is a temporary pass back to the land of the living to help Freki. The gods favor me because of my association with you. I must return to my eternal sleep soon."

"But you can't!" he said. "Don't you know how much I've missed you?"

"And I have missed you too, elsker." she said. "If there was a way that I could come back permanently, you know that I would. I am grateful for this time that we have together now. Is that Margaret with you?"

"Yes." he said "How do you know about her?"

"From where I sit now, I see all." she said. "She has been given the gift of eternal youth. Like Lagertha."

"Hmm." he said. "I just thought she was travelling through time."

"The gods rewarded her for her ordeal with Brenda." she said. "I do not blame Brenda for what she did. She had to, it was fated. It was all decided before we were born."

"That's what Idun is always saying." he said.

"So much was decided for us ahead of time." she said. "Even though it was short, I am eternally grateful for our time together."

She started flickering a little. It was very strange. Now she was fading from view, getting fainter and fainter.

"What's happening?!" he asked. "Why are you disappearing?"

"My time here is over." she said. "My job is done. Never forget Jeg elsker dig, my sweet Gardi."

She was barely visible now. Her voice was also fading.

He reached out for her and got nothing but air.

"NO! NO! COME BACK!" he shouted.

The other Vikings looked at him curiously. None had seen the exchange, in fact none had even seen Astrid. It was as if the only ones who could see her were Freki and Gardi…and Margaret.

"What's the matter, pop?" asked Baldur.

He looked at Freki. He was so engrossed in his conversation with Margaret that he wasn't aware of what had happened.

Why did she have to go? It seemed like a form of torture. He had regretted leaving that whole time he was in England, then he came back and she was dead. He was getting used to strange things happening, but this was just cruel.

Suddenly he heard a voice in his head, it was Astrid.

"I am sorry to leave so suddenly." she said. "I am always with you, we may talk this way at any time. All you need to do is think of me. Your son needs you now. Farewell, elsker."

"Did you see that?" he asked.

"No, we were talking to Margaret." he said. "Why didn't you tell me who she was?"

"You remember her?" he asked.

"No, but he did." said Baldur. "Actually I think we realized it at the same time. But you know that Freki's always been a little quicker than me. I've been talking to her for a week, and the best I figured out was that she was familiar."

"When I saw you, I started thinking about when we were little." said Freki. "Then it all just came together. I still can't figure out how she's so young."

"She has been blessed by the gods." said Gardi. "As has your sister."

"Yeah, about that." he said. "She hasn't exactly filled me in."

"That is something that it will be up to her to tell." he said. "You should have seen how *I* was after I got my gift."

"Yeah, we've heard all of the stories, pop." he said. "I guess I'll go find her now so I can get the lowdown."

He looked at Freki. He knew that his son was in trouble, and according to Astrid, she was here to help him. He wondered if it worked.

"Are you okay?" he asked.

"A lot of strange shit has been happening lately, dad." he said.

"Welcome to my world." he replied.

"So that was her?" he asked.

"Yes." he said. "That was your mother. She was a wonderful woman. The best."

"You say that like she's not coming back." he said.

"She's not." he said.

"You sound sure." he said.

"After a while you get a feel for these things." he said. "She said she came back to help you. What's that all about?"

"I may have gotten a little lost." he said. "I may still be a little lost. I'm trying to find my way back."

"Keep an open mind." he said. "It must have been serious for *her* to come back. I know that you've done things differently since you've been here. Try to remember where you came from."

"I know, it's just that...I don't know. I've learned a lot of things since I've been over here." he said. "I've learned how land is formed. I've learned about the stars, and not just the constellations. I even learned to read, dad."

"So did I." he said. "A few years back."

"Really?" he said. "How did that happen?"

"When you live forever, you get bored." he said. "Idun suggested it. She thinks I'll need it in the future, and she's never wrong about that kind of stuff."

Idun! He hadn't heard that name in a while. Was he really going to get back into all of this? He *had* made a promise...but just to think about it!

He had developed a theory that the simplest answer was most often correct. The fewer complications there were, it simply made any solution easier to explain. Could this be an argument for the gods?

To think about it in this way would make it easier to accept. There was even a little science and logic involved.

Dad really learned to read! He was always smart. Freki always assumed that he got his natural curiosity and instinct to learn from him.

He didn't have any idea about his mother, except what his father and Brenda told him. It hadn't really occurred to him that he could have gotten some of it from her. She had, just by getting him to agree to a couple of bets, gotten him to return to his wife, meet with her, and consider the Norse gods again. And he thought that *he* was smart!

"Do you know what's happening over here?" he asked.

"Unfortunately, yes, son." he said. "None of the crew know yet, but the mission is doomed."

"How do you know?" he asked.

"I've been given the gift of second sight." he said. "It's never wrong."

"I had a dream yesterday." he said. "I dreamt that Guðrum got cornered by Alfred and lost the battle. He surrendered, and gave him some concessions."

"You know what your mother always said about dreams, don't you?" he asked.

"Yeah, I know, I know." he said. "There's no such thing as 'only a dream'."

"She's right you know. I never noticed it until after she told me." he said. "Once she told me I started to pay attention...well, not right away, but after I saw correlations to my waking life I started to pay attention. It's fascinating."

"I never really thought about it." he said. "I had a weird one about Alfdis a while back."

"How is she?" he asked.

"You're not going to believe it. She's back with the Norse gods. My mother was actually the one who told me before it happened." he said. "How did she do that? She also talked me into a few things that had pretty long odds of happening."

"All I can tell you about that is that you should probably take everything she says very seriously." he said. "Your mom doesn't fuck around. She tells it like it is. And she always knew when I was lying."

"She seemed to know that I was in a...I guess you could call it a semi-receptive state." he said. "Hell, she may have even been the one to put me there. A lot of strange things were happening. I thought someone drugged me at this party I went to. I still haven't ruled out that possibility. I made her a promise. I *want* to believe."

"Just keep an open mind, son." he said.

Again with the open mind, he thought. Do they think I have a closed mind, just because I don't jump in with both feet? Do I have to blindly follow them into fantasy land?

"You don't have to jump in with both feet, son." he said. "You don't have to blindly follow us anywhere. We only want you to consider *everything*. Remember Scandinavia. Remember Denmark. Remember what it was like before you came to this strange land."

His father had repeated the exact same words he was just thinking.

"How did you do that?" he asked.

"I've picked up a few tricks since last we met." he said.

Freki heard the words, yet he didn't see his father's lips moving. How did he do *that*?

"Did you just…?" he asked.

"*Did I?* Don't worry about it, Freki." he said. "After all, there has to be a scientific explanation for all of it."

"I'll think about it. dad." he said. "Alfdis is convinced that we should go back to Denmark. She thinks that there will be nothing left for us here after this is over. What would you think about that?"

"I would love to have you back, son, but it might not be safe there either." he said. "We may have to go somewhere else entirely."

"Why?" he asked.

"Guðrum is not only going to surrender to Alfred, he is also going to give him some concessions." he said. "One of which is that he's going to become Alfred's adopted son. He will also convert to Christianity. His Christian name will be Æthelstan. Even after everything that has happened, the people still love him in Scandinavia. You're a smart man, I'm sure you can figure out the rest."

"After he converts, they convert." he said.

"Not all of them, but enough." he said. "If there's a majority of Christians in Scandinavia…or even half, how much will my life be worth?"

"I don't care where you go, dad, I want to come with you." he said. "It's been too long."

Gardi got up and gave him a hug.

"I was hoping you would say that." he said. "Nothing would make me happier."

"We'll play it by ear." he said. "Your new tricks are pretty convincing, but I need more time."

"Just keep an open mind." he said.

* * *

She looked at her skeptically. She was definitely talking the talk. She was saying all the right things, but this was the same woman who tried to convert her last year.

"What about your kids?" she asked.

"Magna and Erika have been wanting to move back to Denmark for the last 6 months." she said. "Aesir has been with Alfred's army for the last year, but I still have hope. Marta is just happy to be with us, whatever the circumstances."

"Marta?" she asked.

"Oh, right. I forgot to tell you. I changed her name." she said. "I couldn't very well have a daughter named Kirsten, could I?"

Daddy was right...again. She had to admit that she was a little jealous. To know what was going to happen in advance. What a useful skill!

I suppose I could just cheat and go into the future. An image of Danu flashed in her head, arms folded powerfully in front of her with *those eyes*. She shuddered a little.

"If you're not serious, you're putting on a hell of an act." she said. "Welcome back, Alfdis."

"Thank you, Lagertha." she said.

She stepped forward and gave her a hug.

"What about Freki?" she asked.

"I'm still working on him." she said. "The rest of the family showing up ought to make it easier, especially your father."

"I've had some dealings with them too...the gods." she said.

"Really?" she said. She could barely contain her excitement. "Tell me all about it!"

"Well...nothing as exciting as my father, and I'm still learning. I'm sometimes able to travel through time...if I do it right. I've made a lot of mistakes." she said. "My teacher is kind of a hard ass. Her name is Danu, and she's a Celtic goddess. I've also been granted eternal youth. But I can still die."

"Danu. I've heard of her in passing since I came here. Nothing good, but you must consider the sources." she said. "She comes from the land west of here, across the sea called Eire. I hear she's very powerful."

"That's the one." she said. "She's actually Odin's mother."

"How could that be?" she asked. "Odin is a Norse god."

"Apparently they're interchangeable." she said. "It's like *everyone* has the same gods, but they call themselves something else depending on where they are."

"So who is *our* Danu?" she asked.

"We don't have one. The Celts have a lot more gods than we do." she said. "Consider yourself lucky you don't know her. She can be a real bitch."

"Still, to communicate with the gods." she said. "It must be exhilarating."

"Idun is much cooler." she said. "Unfortunately, Danu is my mother. Well…Brenda was still my mom, but she is my goddess mother. It's hard to explain."

"You talk to *Idun* as well?" she asked.

"Not as often." she said. "Occasionally she wants to see me for some reason, but most of the work I do is with Danu."

Should I be saying all of this? Was that one of the rules? Oh, well, it's too late now.

"Little Lagertha!" she said. "I'm proud of you!"

"You have a lot of nerve calling me 'little Lagertha' when I stand a foot taller than you." she said.

"Oh, no." she said. "I didn't mean any offense. I was talking in terms of age. I remember when you actually *were* little."

"Well, I'm not little anymore." she said. "Do you have any plans to help my half-brother?"

"It's a work in progress." she said. "It helps to have two living examples right here."

"We will try to help." she said. "I have confidence. He's a smart man, but it might just take some time. I guess we can consider ourselves lucky that you didn't convert him to the false god."

"He can't be converted to anything, believe me, I tried." she said. "What happened here?"

She stroked Lagertha's left cheek.

"It's a long story." she said. "Trust me when I tell you that he got the worst of it."

She looked down at her reflection in the water. It was going to leave a nasty scar, Arve had opened up a 2 inch gash in her cheek. She looked a little closer. Well, maybe not quite that bad. On closer inspection it was an inch...inch and a half tops. Still it would be noticeable. It looked worse now than it would when it healed, but there would be a scar.

Maybe a conversation starter. Or a warning about what happens if you cheat. As if they weren't scared enough of her. Would she ever be able to hold onto a man without killing him?

* * *

"So...ah...I've been thinking about *things*...a lot." he said.

"Yeah?" he asked "What things?"

"Well, you think about things when you get older." he said. "Shit, I'm no good at this. Maybe because I've never done it before. Freki, I just want to say...well...do you remember when we were younger?"

"Probably better than you do." he said.

He looked like he knew what he wanted to say, but he just couldn't get it out.

Freki was pretty sure he knew what was coming next, but he chose to make him say it *himself*, no matter how much squirming he had to do. He needed to do it himself, or else it wouldn't mean as much. Of course, Freki was also enjoying the show. He had never seen his half-brother like this.

"Not when we were little, but later." he said. "When we sailed with pop."

"I remember everything." he said. "Is there something you want to say?"

"Well, it's like this." he started. "Do you remember how we fought...and pillaged?"

"Very well." he said. "You seemed to enjoy yourself quite a bit."

"I did." he said. "But that's not the point. The point is...well, do you remember how things were?"

"I think we've established that." he said.

Baldur looked at him. He just isn't going to make this easy. I guess I deserve it. There was no possible way that he hadn't figured out where this conversation was leading.

"Well...I've learned a lot since I have gotten older, and I know a little more about the human condition. I guess you could say I've mellowed with age. What I've been trying to say, admittedly badly, is that I was an asshole back then." he said. "For all I know, I still am. I didn't feel it at the time, but I feel bad for the way I treated you, and I hope that you can forgive me."

"There is no reason to apologize, brother, all is forgiven. I forgot about all of that a long time ago. We have always been different people, but we have an amazing father in common." he said. "I must admit that I knew this was coming, yet I let you twist in the wind for a few minutes...It was quite entertaining."

"Who's the asshole now?" he asked, chuckling.

"I never held it against you." he said. "As I said, we are two different people. I had fun planning the battles with dad, anyway."

"So how are things?" he asked.

"Honestly, things are pretty strange." he said. "For a while there I thought maybe our water was spiked with some kind of hallucinogen, but that's seeming less and less likely."

"How is Alfdis?" he asked. "Is she still worshipping the false god?"

"That's part of the strangeness." he said. "She did a complete reversal a few days ago. She even changed Kirsten's name to Marta...a good Scandinavian name, she said."

"That's crazy." he said. "Pop called it. He said she would be back with the true gods again. And what about you?"

"I'm not there yet." he said.

"What happened to you?" he asked. "You were so devoted."

"I grew up." he said.

Baldur decided to let that one go. The old Baldur would have punched him in the face. Was he implying that they were all children?

"Do you have any grandchildren yet?" he asked.

"Not yet, but there's one on the way." he said. "Erika. Due in 3 months."

"Same here." he said. "Brenda. She has a little longer than that to go. You'll still be a grandfather before me. She's pretty pissed she couldn't come along on this one."

"She shouldn't be." he said. "I'm sure dad told you that it's a waste of time."

"Yeah, we heard." he said. "Keep it to yourself around the crew. They don't know yet, and pop wants to keep it that way. He says we need to set an example."

"I heard the whole retched story. I'm going back with you." he said.

"You don't want to stay in England?" he asked. "The last time we were here you kept saying how much you like it."

"Alfdis wants to go back. So do Magna and Erika." he said. "Marta is too young to know any better."

"Marta." he said. "That *is* a nice name. Do you ever think you can come back? To the gods?"

"I can never say never." he said. "I lost a bet that demands that I give it serious consideration."

"Really?" he said. "To who?"

"You're going to laugh." he said. "My mother."

"Your *mother*?" he said. "You mean the one who died delivering you in childbirth?"

"Welcome to my world." he said. "Now you can see why I think the water was spiked."

"I hate to point out the obvious, brother, but if you've been talking to your mother, isn't that all the proof you need?" he said. "You've got pop predicting the future with impeccable accuracy, your wife is back with the Norse gods, and you're talking to your mother who has been dead for the last 54 years."

"Oh, and I've been talking to animals." he said.

Baldur rolled his eyes.

"Do you need me to kick your ass and wake you up?" he said. "Everyone I know has been touched by the gods except me! Even my atheist brother!"

"There could still be a logical explanation for all of this." he said.

"And what about Margaret?" he asked. "Is there a logical reason that she still looks 25 after all of this time? She should be in her 70s, hell, maybe even her 80s by now. She looks younger than Lagertha!"

"I need all of the facts to make an educated analysis." he said.

"The facts are that the gods are *all over* this family!" he said. "How can you not see that?"

"I think differently than the rest of you." he said. "You see magic, I see science."

Gardi walked up.

"I hate to break up this little meeting of the minds, but we need to get going." he said. "Lagertha spoke to Danu, and she said that there is still a chance. Are you with us, Freki?"

"Who's Danu?" he asked.

"An ancient goddess." he said. "She is Odin's mother."

19

Asgard

"What did you do?" asked Odin.

"I did what needed to be done. I lied to her. With that many people knowing the truth, it would only be a matter of time before it got out." she said. "The crew needs to believe that he did everything he could. Things will be hard enough for him as it is. *Everyone* needs to believe there is a chance."

"This may go against their efforts to bring his first son back." said Loki. "That has to be important. You know...the whole first son thing."

He glared at Thor.

"If you're talking about this family, you should remember that you were adopted." he said. "You were the spawn of Farbauti and Laufey the frost giants. You are lucky that my father took pity on you after he destroyed them."

"He was looking for a son he could be proud of." said Loki, snickering.

Thor started raising his hammer, and Danu glared at him. She flashed her eyes and he put the hammer down.

"I can see why you have such trouble getting anything done." she said. "If they were my children I would put them in cages!"

Loki couldn't resist.

"Is that what you did to him?" he asked.

He never saw it coming. First Danu slapped him in the back of the head with the flat end of her sword, followed immediately by Odin straightening him up with a backhand to the face.

Thor let out a loud belly laugh.

Odin looked at him.

"*SILENCE!* Do you want some too?" he asked.

He fell silent.

"I am sorry father." he said.

"Freki is beyond our reach." she said. "I do not understand it with his lineage, but he is a true nonbeliever. He must make this decision for himself. There is nothing that we can do."

"I tend to agree." said Idun. "Freki is the type of man that only trusts what he can see. Why he cannot see what is before him as proof, I cannot explain. As Danu says, it is out of our hands."

"Maybe he just needs a good woman." said Freyja. "I could convince him, I know it!"

"Let us try to stay in the realm of reality." said Odin. "None of us are going down there except for Danu and Idun. I'm sure Freki would be sorry if he knew what he was missing, but he has a good wife who is devoted to us."

"I was hoping that would work." said Danu. "He is a hard case. As I said before, we have done all that we can do. It is up to him now."

"I have faith in Gardi." said Idun. "I have faith in all of them. He is not budging yet, but he is coming back to Denmark."

"And how long will they last there?" asked Loki.

He was just recovering from his injuries.

"It does not matter." said Danu. "He has expressed a desire to go wherever his father does. He misses him. We all know that they will probably have to go into hiding. Maybe this will be just what he needs."

"Does anyone have anything else?" he asked.

Nobody said anything.

"Good. Dismissed." Danu quipped.

* * *

"I don't know if I can get involved with all of that now." he said. "It's just not me."

"Are you blind?" asked Baldur. "How can you not *see*?"

Gardi held up one hand to Baldur.

"It's ok, son." said Gardi. "Freki, you don't have to believe, but can you please help me with a battle plan? You were always the best. I need your help. We just want you with us on this. You don't have to fight, just help me with the logistics."

"What about Alfdis and the kids?" he asked.

"They can go home." he said. "We will get them on the way back through."

"Okay. Here's the plan. We'll continue up the Thames." he said. "If we are going to have any chance at all, we'll need to approach from the north, he won't be expecting that."

"It's good to have you back, son." said Gardi.

* * *

They were getting further and further inland. There was a massive storm raging overhead, with thunder crashing and lightning illuminating the sky. Huge drops of rain splattered on the deck of the boat and some of the rain was actually moving sideways with the wind.

"Thor is angry." said Porunn.

Porunn was a very attractive brunette girl who was about 19 or 20 years old. Gardi had let her come along because she reminded him of Brenda. She was also incredibly accurate with a bow and arrow, and lethal with a sword. She was a natural warrior like...well, like Brenda.

"That is called thunder and lightning. I know that you have been taught that it is Thor, but lightning is actually a flash of light created by electrical discharge. A cloud that produces lightning will tend to also have rain." said Freki. "The precipitation process within a cloud is the reason lightning occurs. As ice and water develop in clouds there is an electrical buildup. Lightning occurs to balance the electrical buildup between the clouds and the ground. Thunder is created by the rapid expansion of air. Some people believe that it is the sound of two clouds crashing together."

"I believe that that the simplest answer is most often correct." said Porunn. "What you said was interesting, but a little too complicated. You know…the fewer complications, the easier it is to explain. I'm Porunn. Who are you?"

He couldn't believe it. This girl had just recited one of his scientific theories almost word for word, and used it against him!

"I'm Freki." he said.

"Oh. You're the first son." she said.

She was actually talking to one of Gardi's children! She had tried to talk to his other children, but they never seemed to have the time.

"Don't believe everything you hear about me." he said. "Just because I don't believe in the gods doesn't mean I'm stupid."

"I haven't heard anything." she said. "As far as you're concerned, I'm tabula rasa. You can write whatever you like on my slate."

"You know Latin?" he asked.

"Paulo." she said.

"Michi nunc, paulo." he said.

"So we have a little secret." she said. "I don't know how much of a conversation I could manage, but I'm willing to try."

"We could practice together." he said.

"I would like that." she said. "So why do you not believe?"

"It's a long story." he said. "I've been here for the last 8 years. I've learned a lot. The gods don't make sense anymore."

"Is that the problem?" she asked. "They don't have to make sense! Everything doesn't have to be explained."

"I need proof." he said. "It bothers me if I can't logically explain something, if I can't see it with my own eyes."

"You bloviated about electricity for about 30 seconds, do you know how that works?" she asked.

"In theory." he said.

"Ahh, but can you *see* it? Can you *prove* your claims about lightning and thunder?" she asked. "Can you prove that it *isn't* Thor pounding his hammer? Or do you just love the sound of your own voice?"

This girl isn't pulling any punches! She's not intimidated at all.

He had never met anyone who could make him feel like a fool so quickly. And this girl was younger than 3 of his kids!

"I don't know what to say Porunn." he said. "I've never heard it put quite so simply and elegantly. I guess some things are meant to be accepted with faith."

"Oh, don't change for me." she said. "I'm just a stupid little girl. All I ask is that you keep an open mind."

"You may be many things, Porunn, but you're anything but stupid." he said. "I may have met my match."

"Don't give up so easily." she said. "We have plenty of mental sparring to do yet. It's nice to find someone as intelligent as you. There aren't that many of us around."

"I'm glad that we've met as well." he said. "I'm coming back after this is all over, and I'll need someone to talk to."

"Do you know how to read?" she asked.

"Yes, do you?" he asked.

"I'm learning." she said. "They brought some books back on the last raid. My father bought a slave who knows how. She started to teach me, but she died of pneumonia. I picked up enough to keep going."

"I can help." he said.

"I would like that." she said.

"We should probably try to get some sleep." he said. "It could be a long day tomorrow...I'm still not convinced that there's anything we can do."

"Oh? Why?" she asked.

"I had a dream the other night." he said.

"Oh...so you believe that you can predict the future based on experiences in your unconscious mind, yet you cannot accept the gods?" she asked.

"You're forgetting that what I believe all took place in my mind." he said.

"The infallible brain of Freki Gardisson, eh?" she said. "You know dreams are not just the subject of scientific speculation. They are also represented extensively in Norse culture...as are the *gods*."

"I don't know what I believe, is that better?" he said. "I just think that we're going to be too late to save Guðrum. I think that this trip is a waste of time."

"I don't." she said. "If not for this trip, we may never have met. Perhaps that is the entire reason this happened. Maybe the gods wanted us to get together."

"If that's true, I would have a hard time arguing with them." he said. "Do you really believe that they're that devious?"

"Why are you asking me?" she said. "You don't even believe in them."

"I think I just said I don't know *what* I believe." he said.

"Keep an open mind, Freki." she said. "That's all I ask."

"Bonum nocte." he said.

"Bonum nocte. This isn't over." she said. "Until tomorrow."

"Until tomorrow." he echoed.

* * *

She was swimming effortlessly through the river. It was one of her favorite things to do.

To be out here, in nature, by herself, no gods to worry about, no subjects. It was the most relaxing thing that she could do. Nobody knew where she was. That would be important later on, with the work she must do tonight. As powerful as she was, *this* must remain a secret. Everyone must believe that it is *exactly* what it looks like.

She wondered if they would have had this problem if that idiot hadn't gone to the other side. It certainly had to influence Freki. She figured that she made him go to church with her, and he started questioning the true gods. She had seen it before.

The stories about Jesus were pretty far out there, and all it took was for Freki to question those stories, and the next thing he was doing was questioning his own beliefs.

She really hoped that this would work. Freki deserved better. She had been working on this since before they left Skagen. She had put the girl there. She gave her wisdom. She was pleased with what she had seen so far.

She knew that this eventuality was possible. That was why she did what she did, and why she would do what she needed to do tonight.

That whole excuse to the other gods about the reason she lied to Lagertha was part of the plan as well. She needed them to be apart.

She got out of the water as a lightning crashed on the southern horizon. Thunder roared loudly, and rain splattered hard against her naked body. She left her clothes, but grabbed her sword. She started walking up the path towards the house.

The house was dark when she got there, but the lightning was almost constant, and her eyes had adjusted to the night, so she could see clearly.

She was sure that nobody inside knew what was coming. It didn't matter either way, they would have no chance.

Would it cause him some pain? Undoubtedly. But the little one would be there to pick up the pieces.

She had done everything in her power to make sure that all of them were there. The son was off fighting with Alfred's army, but she would take care of him later.

She reached out and grabbed the door. She ripped it in half as though it was parchment. She walked in and found the older daughters first. They would be the most danger, not that she had *anything* to worry about.

Erika and Magna were sleeping in one corner, and Erika had stirred with the noise of her destroying the door. She easily slid her sword through her neck and did a swift uppercut through her head. She was dead before she could make a sound.

Magna was still sleeping soundly, so she went over and straddled her. She woke with a start, and Danu held her finger to her lips.

"Shhh! Must not wake mother and baby." she whispered.

Magna looked up at her in horror and tried to speak, but all that came out was a weak gasp. Danu reached back as far as she could and punched her in the nose. *Through* the nose was probably more accurate. Her fist rested on the back of Magna's skull, as blood and brains oozed out between her fingers and pooled in the hollow.

She went to Marta and quickly and quietly slit her throat. She was dead without even waking up.

She regretted what she had to do to the children, but it was all part of the message. He needed all of them to be gone in any case. And it had to be believable.

She sauntered up to Alfdis. This was the part that she would *not* regret. She sat on her stomach and slapped her face hard.

Alfdis awoke in shock. She looked up at Danu, and knew immediately that she was a goddess. She frantically wondered what she had done to offend her.

"It was the conversion to the false god." she said. "And now you want to come back like all is forgiven. We might have been okay with that if you hadn't fucked Freki up so bad."

"I didn't mean it!" she said. "I swear!"

"Did not mean it?" she asked, raising an eyebrow. "Is that why you wanted to have your marriage annulled? You felt that it was invalid because you were married before false gods? Or maybe you when you named your daughter after him? Or when you sent your only son away to fight in the Alfred's army. Onward Christian soldiers indeed!"

"But I came back!" she said. "I can bring him back too, I know it! Please give me another chance!"

"You are more of a detriment than a help. You always have been." she said. "Your daughters are dead. Your son will be dead before the sun sets on this day. It is a pity, because they were all innocent in this. They all had a quick death, as will Aesir, and I have made sure that they will all go to the paradise of their choosing. You on the other hand…"

"My babies are gone?" she said.

"Where was your concern for them when you were laying down with the false god?" she said. "You have done them harm as well. You have destroyed this family, yet you beg for mercy?"

She had figured out by now that this was Danu. She didn't even know how to begin to negotiate with her. She wasn't a Norse god, so she wasn't familiar. Lagertha was right, she thought. This one is a bitch.

"When she told you I was a bitch, she said it out of *respect.*" she said. "Unlike you, that girl is smart. I think I've heard enough out of you."

She reached into her mouth and grabbed her tongue. Although most humans had trouble getting a grip, her hand was like a vise. With a swift motion, she ripped it out by the roots. She threw it hard against the wall, and it stuck, then slowly slid down the distance to the floor.

Danu surveyed the room until she found what she was looking for. In the corner against the wall was a broom. She walked over and broke it in two.

"Your daughters won't feel this, because they are already dead." she said. "I *will* have to violate their corpses, however, after I'm done with you. A regrettable part of my task tonight, but it has to look believable. You, however, will feel every inch of it."

Alfdis tried as hard as she could, but she couldn't make a sound without her tongue. Her eyes were wide with terror as she made weak attempts to protest.

"Oh, be quiet! Sit back and enjoy it! I am kidding of course. You are not going to enjoy this even a little bit." she said "Tonight, you will suffer even more than your hero, Jesus Christ. I have heard all of the stories, yet I don't recall one where he gets fucked in the ass by a broom handle."

She proceeded to rape Alfdis with the broom handle and go back to the girls and do the same, trying to be much more humane about it, yet it was still a postmortem insult. She reminded herself that it had to be this way. A few lives for the greater good. It was a simple decision.

When she was done, she took the sharp end of the broom handle and stabbed Alfdis several times in the chest. She didn't use her sword, because Alfdis didn't deserve that kind of death. She could tell by the flow of blood that Alfdis would be dead within the hour. She knew that she was in agony, and that made it so much better.

"Enjoy your last few minutes of pain." she said. "This will be *nothing* compared to how it is going to be where you are going."

She reached into her chest cavity and covered her hands with blood. She started writing on the walls.

She wrote:

"Go home heathens! There is only one true God!"

"To all who would worship the false gods, this is what happens!"

Then she drew a crude cross on the wall with the blood.

Satisfied with her handiwork, she left the house. She walked back to the river and jumped in to wash all of the blood off. She swam for about an hour, then came out and got dressed.

Now to find Alfred's army.

* * *

They got far enough inland to dock the boats and go on foot. They started walking, and crossed paths with a group of soldiers from Alfred's army. Freki went up to them to try to figure out what was happening. He knew their language, and he looked like a local. He talked with them briefly, then came back to Gardi.

"What's going on?" he asked.

"It's just as you said." he said. "Right down to the last detail. They have fled Wessex. Guðrum is coming back next week with 30 of his officers to be baptized. I'll give you 3 guesses as to what his Christian name is going to be, and the first 2 don't count. The adoption will happen at the same time. Alfred is giving Æthelstan the much smaller territory of East Anglia. It's too late. How did you know, dad?"

"It's a blessing and a curse." he said. "Lagertha! Baldur! Bjørn! Get your crews together! We're having a meeting. At the top of the hill in a half hour."

He took Freki aside, away from the others.

"Do you know what this means, son?" he asked.

"I think it means we're going back home." he said.

"That's not all." he said. "It's entirely likely that we-I will need to disappear. It might mean going far away from Scandinavia. I would understand if you don't want to come."

"Nobody knows the future, dad." he said. "For now, I want to stay with you. If this country is going Christian, I want no part of it."

"I could argue that some people actually do know the future." he said. "After all, I just proved it."

"I don't know what that was, but I am not convinced that you are clairvoyant." he said. "I'm sure that there is a logical explanation."

"Once you figure that out, let me know." he said. "We're going back to Denmark, but it might just be to get our people. I have heard of lands to the north, and even lands further west. We may have to begin a whole new settlement."

"I'm in as long as I can bring some books." he said. "Alfdis said she wants to learn to read. It would also not hurt for others in the group to learn."

"I can help you with that." he said. "I hope this is all okay with her. After all, she just abandoned the false god, and came back to us. This much change might be too much for her."

"She'll come even if it's kicking and screaming." he said. "Or she won't. Before all of this, we were on the verge of divorce. Whether she comes or not will not affect my decision either way."

"Are you *sure*, son?" he asked. "You've been married for more than 30 years."

"A lot of it is more complicated than you might think." he said. "You probably wouldn't understand. We have grown apart. She doesn't think as I do. Sometimes it seems that she doesn't think at all."

"Look who you're talking to." he said. "I'm on my 5th wife now. Number 6 is almost certainly lurking around somewhere. You don't have to tell me about the pitfalls of marriage."

"Of course, dad." he said. "Sometimes it feels like I'm older than you psychologically because of your condition. I sometimes forget that you're actually 82."

"My condition." he said. "I'm sure there is a logical explanation for that as well. When you figure it all out, please explain it to me. *Like I'm a 2 year old*, because it's probably beyond my knowledge."

"I don't mean to sound like I know everything, because I don't." he said. "You're a smart guy. Probably smarter than me. The world fascinates me.

I always want to learn more. That's why I have such a hard time believing."

"I know, son." he said. "There isn't any time limit. As much as people might pressure you, you must do this in your own time. That's the only way it will ever work. If you do it for someone else, that's not believing."

"Thank you for understanding." he said. "I'll talk it over with Alfdis after we pick her and the kids up. I'm sure we can find something that works for everyone. I really *do* love her."

"I know you do, son, and I know that this hasn't been easy." he said. "I'm afraid that your natural curiosity is a gift from me. I never thought it would take you down *this* road, but I'm glad you're looking for the truth. I'm just glad that you and I are together again. I've missed you terribly."

I've missed you too, dad." he said. "I love you."

"I love you too, son." he said.

20

It was pitch black. Her wolf senses were on high alert. She had picked up his scent an hour ago. They were on their way back to Alfred's kingdom from battle.

She walked up to the tent. It wasn't ideal for what she *really* wanted to do. There were too many other soldiers around.

She knew that Aesir had fallen under his mother's influence, so he wasn't as culpable as she was, but he *had* joined the opposition's army. He *had* killed Vikings. If she could knock him unconscious undetected, she could drag him out into the forest and take her time with him. No, perhaps a little magic is in order, she thought. She didn't use it much on humans, but this was the perfect time.

She slipped into the tent and counted the men. There were 4 of them, including Aesir who was in the northwest corner. She reached into her pouch and took out a tiny vial. She poured the powder into her left hand and sprinkled Aesir liberally with it. She took another vial of clear blue liquid and doused the others with it.

"Sleep well, my darlings." she said. "You will remember nothing when you wake, except for your guilt."

She walked up to Aesir and bashed him in the face with a large tree branch. He awoke with a start, and opened his mouth to scream, but nothing came out.

"What is the matter little man?" she asked. "Does the cat have your tongue?"

She punched him in the face again.

"You desert your heritage? Your people?" she said. "And for what? To worship a false god, who allows himself to be humiliated? Nailed to a cross?"

He held up a hand in protest. She quickly lopped it off and smacked him in the face with it.

"What is the appeal? I really want to know." she said. "How is such a god to be admired? He does not even defend himself! He actually helps them carry the instrument of his death to the top of the hill."

"Why?" she asked. "Oh…right…the spell. You will not be able to speak for the next 6 hours, which is to say that you will never speak again. I cannot allow you to live. You and your mother have held Freki back long enough."

She ripped off his shirt and pulled out her dagger.

"I bet you would like this to be a cross, right?" she said. "If I had one handy, I might just crucify you. Those Romans had a few things right. They actually worshipped the true gods, at least until Constantine came along."

She started carving into his chest.

"Do not worry, Aesir." she said. We are going back to your roots. Back to a time before you came to this evil land."

She was careful to cut deep enough that there would be no mistake what it was, even with all of the blood.

"There! Even Thor would be proud! A perfect Hammer! Unfortunately for you, this will not be enough to get you into Valhalla. You lost out on that journey long ago." she said. "You *will* be reunited with your mother, though. It will not be a happy reunion, I am afraid. Where you are going there will be no joy. It is an appropriate punishment for the kind of treason you have committed."

She was getting bored. Time to end this. She took the dagger and severed his jugular vein, careful to aim the flow of blood away from her handiwork.

Next she took the branch and placed it into the hand of one of the other soldiers, then she put the dagger in another's hand. In the morning they would 'remember' brutally murdering Aesir and carving up his chest. Their reason would be that his father was a Viking.

* * *

"Unfortunately, our cause here is lost." he said. "Guðrum has surrendered. He will convert to the false religion within the week." he said. "He will also accept Alfred as his adoptive father. His Christian name will be Æthelstan. We will have far fewer holdings in this country. He is giving Æthelstan East Anglia, a small province to the northeast of Wessex. As his adopted son, Æthelstan will be powerless to oppose him. As a Christian, he is a threat to us all. We will go back to Denmark and regroup. There is nothing more we can do here. That is all."

There was some murmuring amongst the crowd. Many of them were talking about the conversion. Gardi was right to be worried. Even after everything that had happened, Guðrum was still popular amongst his men. Only time would tell how bad it was.

They were sailing back to the English Channel as they approached Freki's district. The plan was to stop and get Alfdis and the kids on the way back.

"Oh, she'll come." he said. "After what has happened with Guðrum? I believe her. I think she's really back on board with the Norse gods. There's no way she's staying here."

"And what about you?" she asked. "Where do you land on *that*?"

"I'm still undecided." he said.

"You are the perfect example." said Porunn.

"Of what?" he asked.

"A man who is too smart for his own good." she said. "Evidence abounds all around you, yet you struggle to find a logical explanation. I know better than to argue with you. But you are not keeping an open mind. A closed mind misses a lot of things, Freki."

"My mind is not closed." he said.

She rolled her eyes at him.

"Perhaps you don't understand the meaning of the word in this particular instance." she said. "What I mean is that you are not willing to seriously contemplate the possibility that the gods exist. Your mind is *closed* off to that possibility."

"Maybe you're right." he said. "But I still cannot find my way back to where I started."

"Baby steps." she said. "Find something small that you're willing to compromise on."

"Like what?" he said.

"I don't know, maybe the grass." she said. "It's right there, growing effortlessly. Can you explain that?"

"Yes. It starts with the seed which develops roots, and then sprouts come up when there is enough sunshine and water from the rain."

"Yes, but where did the seed come from?" she asked.

"When the grass gets long enough, it develops seeds which blow with the wind to spread the grass around to a larger area." he said.

"Yes, but what about the *original* seed?" she asked. "Where did the seed that started this wonderful process come from?"

"Well...uh...nobody knows." he said.

"What? Something that cannot be logically explained by science?" she said. "Let's start there."

It was a very simple example, but she had him stumped. He understood how plants grow and he knew the process of photosynthesis, but this girl had him stumped on where the first seed came from. *The first seed!* Somehow, He doubted that even Henry would have an answer.

"Are you looking forward to seeing your wife?" she asked.

"I guess so." he said. "We've been through quite a bit lately. It's complicated."

"I have found when people say 'it's complicated' it generally means that it's rather simple." she said. "It's usually something they don't want to talk about, which I would completely understand, or they are afraid that it might ruin their chances at something or someone else...like me."

"Really?" he asked.

"Yes." she said. "You seem comfortable with me, and I know that you have been unfaithful before, so I'm guessing in your case, it's probably the latter."

"And how would you know that?" he asked.

"Really? You don't know? Some might say it's written all over your face." she said. "Fortunately, I know how to read a little, so I can just make it out. Am I wrong?"

"I don't know what to think of you, Porunn." he said. "For one so young, you're quite insightful."

"My mormor used to say I'm an old soul." she said. "So is it true? Do you want me?"

"Your mormor?" he said. "What about your parents?"

"They died when I was little. Mormor raised me." she said. "Answer the question."

"I cannot deny it. I do desire you." he said. "It's not for the obvious reasons. Well, maybe a *little* for the obvious reasons, but you are different. You're smart. You challenge me. More than my wife could ever dream of. In the last two days, we have had more meaningful discussions than I've had with Alfdis in years."

She looked at him demurely and smiled. She was pretty sure that he was willing, she just wanted confirmation.

"We have about an hour before we get back to your territory." she said. "I can keep a secret. Meet me down below."

She got up and headed down there without looking back.

* * *

He could tell that something was wrong as soon as they started walking up the path. *And how do you know that there's something wrong without any proof?* It was Porunn's voice mocking him in his head.

Whether she knew it or not, she really had him thinking. Maybe he could find that elusive 'open mind'.

After all that had happened in the last few days, he didn't even feel guilty about the sex. He actually felt pretty great about it. A young, attractive, intelligent girl is interested in *me*!

He looked down and saw trails of blood on the path. What was going on?

"Do you see this?" he asked.

"Yeah. Everyone be on your guard." said Gardi. "There's no telling where this blood came from. Be ready."

They got to the house and he saw that the door was ripped in half by what must have been a huge animal.

He heard a growl from inside.

"Let me go in first." said Lagertha.

"No way!" said Gardi. "We don't know what's in there."

"I do. Do you remember what Ama and Brun told you?" she said. "I *know* them. Relax."

"Okay." he said. "She's right. She is as one with the wolves."

Freki gave him a strange look.

She walked in and surveyed the scene. It was a massacre. Whoever did this wanted to make a statement.

"Hello, Aiden." she said. "I hope that you have had enough. It's not your fault, but this is my brother's family. Please leave us in peace."

They filed out the back door, which Danu had left open in all of the havoc.

Lagertha looked over her nieces and her sister in law. She looked at the strange markings on the wall. She recognized only one. The cross.

She fell to her knees. Her hatred of the Christians grew even deeper.

I can't let them see me like this. She slowly got up and headed for the door.

"What's going on?" asked Freki. "What happened?"

"You shouldn't go in there." she said.

He pushed his way past her, and burst through the door. He couldn't believe the scene. Why had they done this? Why Alfdis? Magna, Erika...Marta? He couldn't find her immediately. He found her slumped in the corner, her throat slit and blood between her legs.

"WHY?!?!" he screamed.

He had just noticed the writing. Gardi was looking at it too.

"To all who would worship the false gods, this is what happens!" he said.

"And they call *us* heathens." he said.

For some reason, all Freki could think about at that moment was that his father could read.

Lagertha was just making her way back in.

"What are you talking about, daddy?" she asked.

"The writing." he said, gesturing towards the wall.

"Idun told me that it was a skill that I would need someday." he said. "I hope that this isn't the only reason."

My dad can read! How did he do that? *Where does the grass seed come from?* Boomed Porunn.

If he can read, why can't I understand the gods?

Gardi grabbed a shovel from out back and began digging.

"No." said Freki. "I cannot leave them here. Not in this evil place where they were violated so brutally. I wish to bury them at sea."

"Of course, son." said Gardi.

He gathered some branches, and took some sheets to make a stretcher to carry the bodies. They headed back to the boats.

* * *

It was 3 months later, and they were in a place called Iceland. It wasn't icy, in fact it was green a large percentage of the time. The original Viking settler Hrafna-Flóki Vilgerðarson named it Iceland because when he hiked up the mountains, he discovered that Vatnsfjörður fjord had ice in it.

They had to flee Denmark, as expected. The whole family was there, as well as much of the crew including Porunn.

"I was amazed." he said. "I didn't think he could read. That was all I could think about, even with all of the carnage around me."

"It was probably a defense mechanism." she said. "You know? Your brain trying to help you deal with it. It shut down the part that was hurting."

"That sounds a lot like science." he said.

"I don't deny science." she said. "Particularly when it makes you feel better."

"*You* make me feel better." he said. "I don't know how I would have gotten through this without you."

"You probably would have simply denied that there was a problem." she said. "You would have looked for a reason that everything was okay. An explanation. Proof. Remember all that?"

"You're making it sound like I turned into a true believer." he said. "I don't remember *that* happening."

"It's the kind of thing that you *wouldn't* remember happening. You're right where you are supposed to be." she said. "Baby steps, remember? And speaking of babies…"

"What about babies?" he asked.

"I missed my moon." she said.

"You…Really?" he said. "When?"

"It was due a week ago." she said.

"Are you sure?" he asked. "You didn't mix up your weeks?"

"Please." she said. "When have you ever known me to be absent minded?"

"Never." he said. "I wasn't supposed to have any more kids. A very intelligent doctor in England told me that Marta would be my last. I have regretted hearing that ever since…well, you know. I don't have any children left."

"Well, guess what?" she said. "Is this proof? Is this what you need to finally believe?"

"Maybe just for today." he said.

"Sometimes, today is all we have." she said.

"Jeg elsker dig." he said.

"I know." she said.

She couldn't keep a straight face. She started giggling.

"You know I love you too, sweetheart." she said.

"I suppose we ought to get married." he said.

"Such romance." she said.

"I didn't mean…" he said.

"I know what you meant." she said. "The big question is what kind of ceremony will we have?"

He thought about it. He still thought about Alfdis and the girls from time to time. And Aesir. He had gotten word that religious fanatics in Alfred's army had killed his son. Because of him. Apparently they had heard that Freki used to be a Viking.

Now he was going to marry a beautiful young girl and start a new family.

Suddenly an image of a beautiful black haired woman wearing a green dress with a golden helmet with wings resting in the crook of her arm appeared. There was no doubt in his mind that she was a goddess.

He shook his head. Now I'm seeing things, he thought. Is it so impossible? Could all of the stories be true? He couldn't prove it, but he couldn't disprove it either.

"We will have a traditional Norse wedding." he heard himself say.

"Do you mean it?" she asked. "Can we?"

"Of course." he said. "I'm not quite there yet. Well, maybe I am. I don't know…I *want* to believe. I also want you to be happy. Maybe as I prepare for the ceremony, I can get more into the spirit of things. *I want to believe.*"

"Well, this is progress." she said. "I'm impressed. I believe you."

"Porunn, I have been given a second chance at life. A second chance at love." he said. "Perhaps a second chance with the gods. I'm still working towards that. You have made me the happiest man in Iceland. If I have to try to believe for this to work, it is a very small sacrifice."

"I don't want you to feel obligated on my account." she said. "That makes it seem like a burden."

"It's *not* a burden." he said. "I never wanted anything so much in my life. Please just be patient with me. This could take some time. I want to believe as you do. As I used to believe."

"You have the rest of your life." she said. "And I will be by your side for the duration, no matter what you decide."

Epilogue

Iceland 1066 A.D.

He had been following the campaigns in England for some time now.

For the first time since before the time of Guðrum they had a legitimate chance of regaining power. Edward the Confessor had died, and there was quite a battle to decide who would succeed him on the throne.

One claimant was Harald Sigurdsson of Norway, also known as Harald Hardrada. He had even briefly claimed the Danish throne in 1064. He was getting help from Tostig Godwinson, the new king Harold Godwinson's brother. He was making good progress in England, battling his way to Harold.

Gardi was waiting for Leidolf to make it back from England so he could hear the latest.

In 886, Danelaw was established, pursuant to a treaty between Alfred and Æthelstan. It was a small territory northeast of Wessex. It wasn't actually official, the Vikings were still under English rule. Æthelstan would never admit it, but that is how it was.

Alfred had set it up that way on purpose. Adopting him, making him convert, it was all so he could control him.

They had gone through many years of relative peace, where the Vikings hadn't caused any trouble.

In 1016, Cnut unified the North Sea Empire, ruling over England, Norway, Denmark, and part of Sweden. He ruled until 1035, when his successors inherited the throne.

When Cnut's son Harthacnut died in 1042, it reverted back to the English line in the form of Edward the Confessor. That lasted until he died in 1066.

Now it was up for grabs again, and it looked like Harald Sigurdsson had a legitimate chance of regaining England.

He had seen Leidolf's boat when it was about a quarter of a mile away from the fjord, now he was finally closing in.

"It's him, isn't it, daddy?" asked Lagertha.

"Yes." he said.

"You don't sound too happy about it." she said "Is it bad news?"

"It always seems to be." he said. "I don't even need to talk to him. It's over."

"Are you sure?" she asked.

"Have you ever known him to be wrong?" she asked.

It was Margaret. The two of them had mellowed over the years. They still weren't buddies, but they found a way to make it work.

He pulled the boat up. His face said it all, there was no hiding the disappointment.

"How bad?" he asked.

"He just wasn't the right guy." he said. "They killed both of them. Him and Tostig. He was doing great, then it all fell apart. They went down for the last time at Stamford Bridge."

"He was our last hope." said Gardi.

"Not necessarily." said Leidolf. "There are still some in Denmark that still believe."

"Still some." he said. "Our homeland is Christian. England is Christian. All of Europe is Christian. It's over, Leidolf."

"But we're not Christian." he said.

"We will have to move again soon." he said. "There have been more and more Christian settlers here. We can try to keep to ourselves, but they know who we are."

"Where will we go?" he asked.

"I have heard of lands across the great sea." he said. "South of here, and further west than Greenland. It is wild country, untamed by man."

"When will we go, daddy?" she asked.

"When the weather breaks." he said.

"Let's go back to the village." he said. "We need to plan this thing."

He had populated a most of village of 576 people with his descendants. He still remembered everyone's names. Other settlers came and married members of his family, but most people in the village had some familial tie to Gardi.

* * *

He was up in the mountains. He always came here when he wanted to get away. There was another reason tonight, though. He looked up at the stars. He loved how clear the sky was up here. He went through the constellations as he always did. The Eagle, Frigga's Distaff, Loki's Torch, and Ratatosk. On the eastern horizon were Thjazi's Eyes.

He knew instinctively that she was there.

"I am getting used to you." he said.

"Really?" she said. "It has been 242 years. What took you so long?"

"I have been used to you for a while now." he said. "There are no surprises anymore."

"Perhaps I will have to create one." she said.

"What did you have in mind?" he asked.

"The universe overflows with ideas." she said. "Besides, if I told you, it would not be a surprise."

"Fair enough." he said. "We will leave soon."

"I know, elsker." she said. "But you must go alone. You must leave without telling them."

"Why?" he asked.

"They have made their lives here. In the future, you will not be able to have such a large family. Do not misunderstand me, the gods are thrilled. You have created many descendants." she said "You have been hidden away on this island. It is good that you want to leave. You cannot stay in one place this long. People who do not know you would never understand. You must be more discreet in the future."

"Any suggestions?" he asked.

"I think that you had the right idea." she said. "To the west. There is a new world over there."

"To the west it is, then." he said.

"Of course, you will take Lagertha and Margaret." she said. "You have to let Helga and Frida go."

"Of course you are right." he said. "They deserve to live the rest of their days in peace. I will miss them. I still love them."

"Of course you do, dear." she said. "This is the nature of things. You will have to do a lot of this in the future. It will never get easier."

"I know. After all, I have been around for 270 years now." he said.

"And you have been here for almost 200 of those years." she said. "You should have been gone long ago. You will not be able to do that again. People do not believe in magic anymore. You cannot go more than 15 to 20 years in any one place anymore."

"I knew this time was coming." he said. "I knew it the whole time I have been here. I did not want to leave my family."

"Hold your family in your thoughts, and they will always be with you." she said. "I must go. You must go also. Prepare when you get back. Leave tomorrow. It is the only way."

"Okay." he said.

She was off, screaming across the sky.

Is this what life will be from now on? Going from place to place, never staying more than 20 years?

She was right. He had stayed in Iceland for far too long. West…to a new world.

Made in the USA
Middletown, DE
03 October 2015